Cliff Hawk was a very special man—and he loved
Molly Zaldivar. He had no way of knowing
his love would mean the death of the girl.
But he had set in motion forces of cosmic
power. And because of his love for Molly,
the power he had unleashed would be in-
timately keyed to the person of this one
perfectly imperfect human female.

A star does not understand love, or hate. It
'understands' only life. And even life is not
necessarily life as humans know it.

But Molly had no way of knowing that. None of
them had any way of knowing—once the
star had been created—what it could do,
what it would want, and where they would
end.

Other titles by Frederik Pohl
and Jack Williamson

STARCHILD
THE REEFS OF SPACE

Also available from Ballantine Books.

This is an original publication—not a reprint.

ROGUE STAR

**FREDERIK POHL
JACK WILLIAMSON**

BALLANTINE BOOKS • NEW YORK

First Printing: December, 1969

Cover Painting: Paul Lehr

Printed in the United States of America

BALLANTINE BOOKS, INC.
101 Fifth Avenue, New York, New York 10003

ROGUE STAR

I

The sudden light hurt his eyes and woke him rudely from a dream of Molly Zaldivar. Clutching blindly for support, he found only warmth and yielding softness. A panic sense of dislocation dazed him.

"Monitor Quamodian!"

That sweet, synthetic voice restored his sense of place. The Exion research station. The human habitat on the planet Exion Four. The cybernetic dwelling he had built to share with Molly, before she went away. He was in it all alone, floating in the null-gee capsule of his sleeper, a naked foetus in a pink plastic womb.

"Monitor Andreas Quamodian!" The sleeper's bright robot voice grew more intense. "The speaker has a transfac message for you."

He grunted his hurt protest and clung to his fading dream of Molly. Somehow he had found her.

1

He'd been fighting Cliff Hawk, to take her back. Somehow, unbelievably, he'd been winning . . .

"Monitor, please!"

He squirmed inside the padded cocoon, groping to recover that good feeling. He wanted to recall his breathless sense of triumph over Hawk, his blood-speeding certainty that Molly wanted him to win.

But all the circumstances of the dream vanished as he grasped for them. Painfully awake, he had no idea where in all the clustered galaxies Molly and Cliff Hawk had gone. He couldn't imagine any real-life situation in which he could hope to beat Cliff Hawk, nor could he quite believe that Molly would ever want him to.

His squinted eyes came open on his image in the sleeper's mirror. Too much belly. Too little muscle. A round bald spot on top of his head. He turned away from his soft plump whiteness.

"I wish you hadn't waked me," he muttered at the sleeper. "I'm not on duty. I don't want any calls. Just put me back to sleep."

"But, sir!" the machine reproved him sulkily. "You can't ignore this message. The sender rated it urgent. The index code implies crisis on an inter-planetary scale, with probable danger to billions of your fellow human creatures."

"Great Almalik!" He blinked at the pink folds of pulsating plastic. "Where's the message from?"

"The central zone," the sleeper said. "The local address is Planet 3, Star 7718, Sector Z-989-Q, Galaxy 5 . . ."

"That's Earth!"

"A local name, perhaps," the sleeper said. "We don't record such unofficial designations."

2

"I should know. Earth's my native planet. Give me the message."

"It's coded personal and confidential," the sleeper protested. "You'll have to accept it from the speaker."

"Get me up," he said. "I'll accept it."

While the machine was getting him up, he tried to imagine who on Earth the message could be from. Not his parents, certainly. They had accepted the symbiotic way of life while he was still a child. Lately they had migrated to a human colony in Galaxy 9. Secure in the Starchurch, they would never need anything from him.

Molly Zaldivar?

Wild hope struck him when he thought of her. Though he had never learned where she and Hawk went from Exion, he knew they were both natives of Earth. Perhaps she had come back home. Perhaps she was through with Hawk. Perhaps she really wanted him!

He smiled fondly at his recollection. Molly Zaldivar, five years ago. A tall lively girl, who sang and accompanied herself on an Earth guitar. A girl loved by many a being on the planets of Exion, where they first met—even though they both had come from Earth.

It was easy for him to know why he loved her: the laughter in her voice, even when she sang the saddest ballads of the old mother world, the skin tones that changed oddly from warmest ivory to tawny gold under the queer shifting light of the triple star. But—half the students did not "hear," at least on the audio frequency range used by human beings; many

3

of them did not see with "visible" light. Yet all were fond of Molly Zaldivar.

The three had been together in the tiny group of Earth people Dr. Scott had gathered to work in his stellar section. Andy Quamodian, already serious, already pudgy, dark and slow. Molly Zaldivar, like a golden flame, her bright hair catching ruddy glints from the red giant component of Exion, her dark eyes flashing the violet light of the dwarf. And— Cliff Hawk.

Even after five years, Quamodian scowled at the thought of Hawk. He was a rogue in the society of men, stranger than any alien at the research station, solitary, brooding, angry. He seldom washed, seldom combed his shaggy black hair, seldom spoke a civil word. Yet somehow Molly had chosen him.

Waiting now for the machine to steam and rise and dry and clothe him, Quamodian darkly pondered Hawk. Both human, both had drifted all the way from Earth to Exion, this farthest outpost star of the whole galactic cluster. But they were different in nearly every other way.

Before the fusorians came, Quamodian's commonplace parents had toiled for their living in a commonplace clothing shop in a commonplace city, but Hawk's ancestors were bold outlaws who roved the reefs of space and defied the old interplanetary empire called the Plan of Man. Muddling through his dull career, Quamodian had relied on logic and method and sheer persistence. Scornful of everything systematic and academic, Hawk played brilliant hunches. A half-trained technician, he had finally challenged Scott for leadership of the stellar project.

Though he sometimes lacked the words to frame his daring intuitions, they were usually correct.

Hawk loved Molly Zaldivar—carelessly and roughly, certain that she would sacrifice her own career for any of his whims. Quamodian worshipped her more humbly—always aware that he was only plodding little Andy Quam. When the time came for Molly to choose, she really hadn't a choice. Of course she took the dark, dangerous man who knew the borderlands of space.

Her choice was not surprising, though the actual sequence of events still puzzled Quamodian. Hawk had somehow quarreled with Dr. Scott about the direction of their efforts in the stellar section to contact rogue stars. When Scott won their final battle, Hawk disappeared, leaving Molly behind.

After a few unhappy months, Molly was willing to sing her sad ballads to Quamodian. That was when he planned the cybernetic house to share with her. Before it was finished, she heard from Hawk. Just what she heard, Quamodian had never learned. The news, whatever it was, had seemed to bring her more terror than gladness. Yet, without explaining anything, she left at once to follow Hawk.

Now, five years later, her abrupt departure was still a painful riddle to Quamodian. It kept throbbing like a bad tooth, something he could neither understand nor forget.

"Ready, sir?" the machine droned. "Up you come!"

With a peristaltic thrust, the floatation field popped him out of his warm cocoon. He swayed for a moment, adjusting to the planet's gravity, and turned to the speaker.

"Okay," he said. "I'll take the message."

"Standard voice identification is required, sir."

"Great Star! You know who I am."

"But you know our procedures, sir," the speaker said. "The full standard voice identification pattern is required before delivery of all transgalactic communications."

"Ridiculous!" he muttered. "Silly red tape."

The machine hummed quietly inside its black synthetic skin. With a scowl of annoyance, he caught his breath and recited the formula:

"Name: Andreas Quamodian. Race: Human. Birthplace: Earth—correction, that's Planet 3, Star 7718, Sector Z-989-Q, Galaxy 5. Organization: Companions of the Star. Status: Monitor. Address: Human habitat, Exion Four, Exion Extragalactic Research Station."

"Thank you, Monitor Quamodian."

The machine clicked and ejected a narrow strip of yellow film. He snatched it eagerly, and peered to see who it was from. Molly Zaldivar!

"Dear Andy—" The film began to quiver in his sweaty fingers. "I hope you can forgive me for leaving you so rudely, because I'm in desperate trouble here on Earth. It's all too complicated to explain by transfac, but I need your help because the Companions here don't believe in rogue stars . . ."

Rogue stars! The phrase brought Quamodian to a painful halt. He wanted Molly to be sending for him because she'd decided that she loved him after all. Not for any other reason.

Besides, he didn't really understand rogue stars. Neuroplasmic theory was familiar to him in an academic way. Theoretically, he knew how the sentient stars perceived, remembered, thought, and acted

—how mass effects induced transcience energy, how bits of information were stored in states of electron spin, how scanning waves flowed through chains of elections in transflex contact, how transcience impulses induced magnetic and electrical and gravitic effects. He respected their tremendous minds, the most retentive and most complex in all the galaxies. He felt a vast admiration for the mellow wisdom of Almalik, the stellar component of the symbiotic citizen that so many human beings had joined. But the rogue stars were something else.

Given its unthinkable intelligence and power, how could a stellar being refuse all fellowship with any other mind? What sort of obsession or psychosis could cause it to close all communication and choose to go its own lonely way?

Quamodian had often listened to debates about that riddle, which was among the basic research problems of Exion Station. He had even discussed it with Molly and Cliff Hawk, in Scott's graduate seminars. He had never heard an answer that made real sense.

"Are you ready to reply, sir?" the speaker was purring. "The sender wants an answer."

"Wait," he said. "Let me finish."

"If you have ever wondered what became of me," the transfac continued, "Cliff Hawk asked me to join him here on Earth. I came because I love him— Andy, I can't help that. I came because I was afraid of what he might be doing here. And I've just discovered that he's doing what I feared. He has learned too much about rogue stars—or maybe too little. Andy, would you believe he's trying now to create a rogue of his own? I need help to stop him.

"Here's what you must do, dear Andy. Get Solo Scott—Hawk's old enemy. I don't know where he is—I tried to reach him at his old address in the stellar section, but he didn't reply. Andy, I want you to find him and bring him to Earth. He's the great rogue star specialist. He'll be able to stop Cliff—and Cliff's dangerous new rogue—if anybody can.

"But hurry, Andy! This is a terrible thing, and I have no hope but you."

Quamodian finished reading with a tired little sigh. Molly's feelings for him hadn't changed, after all. He was still only Andy Quam, a useful little tool when she happened to need him.

"Now, sir?" the speaker droned impatiently. "Will you reply?"

"First," he said, "I want to make a local call. To Dr. Solomon Scott. He used to be director of the stellar section, here on Exion Four."

"Yes, sir." The speaker hummed silently for three seconds. "Sorry, sir," it purred. "Dr. Scott is not available. He left Exion four years ago on a research expedition from which he did not return. He is presumed dead, sir."

"That's too bad," Quamodian said, but a thrill of irrational hope was tingling through him. If Scott was not available, he could go to Earth alone. Little Andy Quam might at last become Molly's rescuing hero! He caught his breath. "Send this answer:

"Dearest Molly, I want to help you but I have bad news. I can't bring Scott. He left Exion Station a year after you did. He was attempting a transflection flight to the vicinity of a rogue—the same one Cliff had discovered, out beyond Exion. He never got back.

"But I'll come, Molly. Because I still love you—in spite of everything. If you want just me, answer at once. I'll get there as soon as I can.

"End of message."

His words flickered across the visual panel as the speaker read them back. He snatched a light-pen and scribbled, "Your devoted Andy," before the small blue tongue of plasma began to lick the symbols away, storing them as variances in electronic spin.

Waiting for Molly's reply, he scowled impatiently. He knew that his signal was already reaching the far-off Earth, as its invisible impulses automatically sought the shortest route along the transcience links between the shifting convolutions of hyperspace, where long light-years were reduced to micromicrons.

The plasma tongue finished and vanished, leaving the message panel blank. The speaker clicked off. The house hummed quietly around him, hushed and tense. He walked the floor around the speaker, watching the flickering symbols of the universal clock.

Panic whispered that Molly wouldn't want him. Not without Scott. She knew that little Andy Quam had never been an actual member of the Exion research staff, but just a sort of guinea pig. Scott had brought him along to test a hunch that his odd location sense was a transience effect, but dropped him from the project when the rogue star research became more exciting . . .

"Monitor Quamodian!" The machine's droning tone startled him. "We have a status report on your transgalactic message."

"What—what does Molly say?"

"There's no answer, sir. We can't contact the addressee."

"Why not?" His voice cracked. "Has something happened to Molly Zaldivar?"

"We have no information, sir."

"Take another message." He tried to swallow the squeaky quaver in his voice. "To Molly Zaldivar. Same address. Message follows: On my way to Earth. Sign it, Andy Quam."

II

Hurried but methodic, Quamodian prepared for his trip to Earth. He called his supervisor for emergency leave, left instructions with the speaker for care of the house, and asked the flyer to stand by. His spirits soared with the levitator which lifted him to the roof pad, but fell again as he stepped outside.

As always happened whenever he left his cybernetic shell, Exion gave him a queasy shock of dislocation. The place was too far from all the other worlds he knew, too alien to any sort of life. Some freak of cosmic chance had flung the triple star far outside the galactic cluster, and the university had chosen it for the research site because no spark of native life or sentience had ever appeared on any of its bodies.

The station staff had reclaimed and terraformed

its twelve dead planets to fit their several ways of life. Those sister worlds were strung across the black sky now, like beads on an unseen string, each aglow with the color of its own synthetic biosphere: supercold liquid helium, frigid methane, hard vacuum, hot carbon dioxide, boiling sulphur.

Exion Four was for the oxygen-tolerant. The human habitat where he lived was only a hasty afterthought—a cragged scrap of crater floor, temporarily pressurized, heated, and humidified enough to allow human survival. Still too thin and cold, its artificial atmosphere was always tainted with hydrocarbons and ammonia escaping from the rocks. Too small to seem like home, the planet turned too slowly.

Shivering, Quamodian hunched himself against the bitter oxy-helium wind. Fighting that first giddy shock of disorientation, he stopped to search that queer sky above the crater cliffs. A tight constriction in his chest relaxed when he found the galaxies—a fuzzy patch of pale light, bitten off by the southward cliffs, fainter than the dimmest planet of Exion.

"Ready, sir?" The flyer opened itself. "Where to, sir?"

"To the regional transport center." He scrambled inside. "I'm in a rush."

The flyer climbed until the violet dwarf peered over the saw-toothed east horizon, dropped back into the dark, and settled toward the lighted ramp outside the transflex cube. The control dome flashed a signal.

"Identification, sir?"

He let the flyer hover while he recited his standard voice pattern and sorted out the documents of his citizenship. The dome extended a long, nimble finger of pale plasma to scan his passport disk, with its endless rows of binary symbols and its holograph of his dark, round head.

"Destination, sir?"

"Earth. That's—wait just a second—that's planet 3, Star 7718, Sector Z-989-Q, Galaxy 5. Route me through the Wisdom Creek station, Octant 5. I'm on emergency business. I need passage at once."

The plasma tendril winked out. Quamodian caught the passport disk as it dropped, stowed it away, then resumed his inching crawl toward the luminous iris of the transflex cube. A long silver tank, no doubt filled with a liquid citizen, was vanishing through the closing gate. Behind it came a multiple creature, a horde of small, bright, black things, hopping and tumbling inside a communal cloud of pale blue mist. A gray-scaled dragon shuffled just ahead of Quamodian, burdened with a heavy metal turret on its back that probably housed unseen symbiotes. Winking crystal ports in the turret peeked out at Quamodian and shyly closed again.

"Sir?" The control dome flashed again. "Have you a reservation number?"

"Great Star!" Impatience exploded in him. "I've got to reach Earth at once. I just received an emergency call. I had no time to arrange a reservation."

"Sorry, sir." The dome's droning regret seemed entirely mechanical. "Intergalactic travel is restricted, as you should know. We cannot approve transit without a reservation based on acceptable priority."

Grumbling, he held up the message from Molly Zaldivar. The slim plasma finger reached down to scan it, hesitated, recoiled.

"Sir, that document is not in the universal language."

"Of course not," he snapped. "It's English. But it ought to be priority enough. Just read it!"

"We have no equivalence data for English, sir."

"Then I'll translate. It's from Earth—that's the mother planet of my race. The sender is a girl—I mean, a youthful female human creature—named Molly Zaldivar. Her message is addressed to me. She's begging for help. She gave the message an urgency index that implies danger to the whole planet . . ."

"Sir!" Ahead of him, the multiple creature had disappeared into the transflex cube. The dragon was lumbering toward the opening iris. "You're delaying transit. I must ask for an actual reservation number now."

"But *this* is my priority!" He waved the yellow scrap of transfac tape. "Molly Zaldivar is in some kind of trouble with a rogue star . . ."

"Sir, that is not an acceptable priority. Please leave the ramp."

"Confound you!" Quamodian shouted. "Can't you get anything through your neuroplasmic wits? This message implies a danger to the whole human race!"

"Sir. The human race is identified in my files as a little breed of barbarians, just recently admitted to the galactic citizenship and still devoid of interesting traits, either physical, moral, or intellectual. No human being is authorized to issue priority for interstellar travel."

"But Molly says we're in danger . . ."

"Sir, please leave the ramp. You may apply to any

acceptable source for a transit priority, on the basis of which we can issue you a reservation number."

"I have no time for that . . ."

The dome signaled no reply, but ominously the plasma tendril thickened and began to spread.

"Wait!" Quamodian cried desperately. "I'm a member of the order of Companions of the Star! Surely you know of them. Our mission is to protect humanity, and other races, too."

"My indices do not show any authorization issued to you for this journey by the Companions of the Star, sir. You are holding up traffic. Please move off the ramp."

Quamodian glanced bleakly at the citizen crowding up behind him: forty tons of sentient mineral, granite-hard, jagged and black, afloat on its own invisible transflection field and impatiently extending its own passport at the tip of a blue finger of plasma.

"Don't shove, Citizen!" he barked. "There's been a misunderstanding. "Listen, Control. Check your records. We humans are allied to the multiple citizen named Cygnus, which is a symbiotic association of fusorians, stars, robots, and men. Its chief star is Almalik—or don't you find sentient stars any more interesting than men?"

His irony was wasted on the dome. "Get out of the line," its signal flashed imperatively. Then, a split second later, "You may wait on the side of the ramp. The multiple citizen Cygnus is listed on our indices. We will call the star Almalik, in Galaxy 5."

Disgruntled, Quamodian switched his flyer out of line, giving up his place to the granite citizen, who passed him with an air of disdain. He hovered impatiently at the edge of the ramp, watching the gate ahead expand again as it swallowed the gray-scaled dragon and its turret of symbiotic fellows.

For a moment Quamodian thought of making a mad dash for the iris aperture, but there was no sense in that. However fast his flyer moved, the dome would be faster, and he would reduce his narrow chance of getting through.

He sat for a time staring blankly out at the horde of beings slowly moving past him on the ramp. At last he shook himself.

"Divert me," he said harshly. At once a more than humanly soprano voice began to sing from somewhere inside the flyer: *"Mi, mi chiamano Mimi. . ."*

"No. Not opera."

The voice fell silent. A holograph of a chessboard appeared on the communications panel, the pieces set up for a game; White's King's Pawn slid forward two spaces and waited for his reply.

"I don't want to play chess, either. Wait a minute. Set up a probability matrix for me. Estimate the chances of the star Almalik granting me a priority!"

"With running analysis, or just the predicted expectancy, Mr. Quamodian?" asked the flyer's voice.

"With analysis. Keep me amused."

"Well, sir! By gosh, there's a lot of stuff you got to consider, like . . ."

"Without the comedy dialect."

"Certainly, Mr. Quamodian. These are the major factors. Importance of human race in universal civilization: low. Approximately point-five trillion humans, scattered on more than a hundred stellar systems in three galaxies; but these represent only about one one-hundredth of one per cent of the total population of universal civilization, even counting multi-

15

ple and group intellects as singles. Concern of star Almalik with individual human Andreas Quamodian, negligible."

"What about the concern of Almalik for the Companions of the Star?" cried Quamodian angrily.

"Coming to that, Mr. Quamodian. Concern rated at well under noise level on a shared-time basis, but inserting the real-time factor makes it low but appreciable. So the critical quantity in the equation is the relevance of the term 'rogue star.' I have no way of estimating the star Almalik's reaction to that, Mr. Quamodian."

"The rogue stars are among the most important phenomena in the universe," said Quamodian, staring out at the ramp. "Exion Station was set up largely to study them."

"In that case—hum—allowing for pressure of other affairs; you haven't kept up with the news, but there have been some unpleasant events reported on Earth—let's see, I give it point-seven probability, Mr. Quamodian. One hundred fourteen variables have been considered. They are respectively . . ."

"Don't bother."

"It's no bother, Mr. Quamodian," said the machine, a little sulkily. They were all moody, these companionship-oriented cybernetic mechanisms; it was the price you had to pay for free conversation.

Quamodian said soothingly, "You've done well. It's just that I'm upset over the danger represented by the rogue star."

"I can understand that, Mr. Quamodian," said the machine warmly, responding at once. "A threat to one's entire race . . ."

"I don't give a hoot about the human race!"

"Why, Mr. Quamodian! Then what . . ."

"It's Molly Zaldivar I care about. Make a note of this, you hear? Never forget it: the welfare of Molly Zaldivar is the most important thing in the universe to me, because I love her with all my heart. In spite of . . ."

"Excuse me, sir," the flyer broke in. "An approaching craft is hailing us."

"Who is it?"

"The operator is your fellow human, Solomon Scott."

"Scott?" He squinted into the glaring terminal lights but saw no approaching craft. "It can't be Scott."

"He's Solomon Scott," the flyer said flatly. "We have positive identification through his standard voice pattern. He entered the air space of Exion Four without official clearance, and the robot guardians are after him. But he says he has an urgent message for you."

III

The hailing craft dived into the terminal lights, grazed the flyer, and crashed to the pavement near the ramp. Jolted out of his seat, Quamodian recovered his balance and blinked at the strange machine.

It looked like something a dragon had mauled. A

great steel globe, battered and fused and blackened. A few twisted projections looked like stumps of lost instruments or weapons. Without wings or jets or landing gear, it seemed entirely unfamiliar until he found traces of a symbol he knew under the scars and rust—the triple-starred emblem of Exion Station.

"It is Scott," he whispered. "That's the environmental pod he left here in. Or part of it."

"Stupid human!" the flyer huffed. "He nearly wrecked us. I'm calling the guardians."

"Wait! He's the man Molly Zaldivar needs on Earth. Read him the message from her. Ask him to help us stop Cliff Hawk from whatever he's doing to create a rogue."

The flyer hummed quietly. Waiting for Scott to reply, Quamodian began to feel ashamed of himself. He couldn't help a dull regret that Scott had turned up to rescue Molly. His own chance was gone, he thought, to be her solitary champion.

"Scott's speaking," the flyer whirred at last. "He says he has an urgent personal message for you. He wants you to come aboard his machine. He says he can't stand outside exposure here."

"What about Cliff Hawk and Molly Zaldivar?"

"He says Cliff Hawk's an arrogant fool. But he says Molly's wrong if she thinks Hawk's research is dangerous. He says the rogue stars are a harmless myth."

"That's not what he thought when he was putting armor plate around that research machine," Quamodian muttered. "Tell him Molly is terrified."

"Scott says she's another fool," the flyer purred. "He says he won't waste time on any crazy chase to

18

Earth. But he's anxious to see you. Will you visit his machine?"

Quamodian's hopes had soared again. If Scott wouldn't come to Earth, perhaps there was still some wild chance for him to be Molly's lone rescuer.

"Uh?" He sank back to hard reality. "Tell Scott I'm coming now."

He scrambled out of the flyer. The terminal was miles above the altitude of the human habitant, and the bitter chill of the thin oxy-helium mix at this level took his breath. He ducked his head and ran for the damaged craft. A valve opened as he reached it, and a tall stranger reached down to haul him into the shadowy air lock.

"Scott?" The wind had taken his voice. "I was looking for Solo Scott . . ."

"I'm Solomon Scott," the stranger rasped. "Come inside."

Quamodian recoiled. The stranger in the lock looked as tall as Scott, but with that their resemblance ended. Scott had been a dark, aggressive, vital man, as strong and ruthless as another Cliff Hawk. This man was gaunt and gray and slow, oddly clumsy in the way he reached out of his steel cave, somehow more mechanical than human.

His dress was equally perplexing. He wore a monkish cowl of thick gray stuff and a long gray robe gathered with a golden chain around his waist. Slung from the chain was a thin golden dagger, which glowed queerly in the dark of the lock.

Quamodian wanted to turn and run. He couldn't understand anything about Scott's arrival. He didn't like the flat glitter of Scott's haggard eyes, or even the greasy spots on the clerical robe. A sour whiff of something inside the globe almost gagged him.

"Andy!" the stranger shouted into the oxy-helium wind. "Come on aboard."

He tried to get hold of himself. After all, he saw no actual danger, and he wanted help for Molly. He grasped the reaching hand, which felt colder than the wind, and scrambled up into the dim steel cell.

"Solo!" He tried to force his stiffened face into a grin. "It's great luck you turned up just now, because Molly Zaldivar is desperate for your expert aid. If you'll read her message . . ."

"Forget it!" Scott's gray claw slapped carelessly at Molly's transfac tape. "Come out of this cold, so we can talk."

But Quamodian hung back, his stomach turned by one glimpse of the gloomy space beyond the haggard man and the inner valve. Filthy rags and torn paper. Tumbled piles of broken scientific instruments. Empty plastic food containers. Dust and rust and human dung.

"What's all this?" He couldn't help shivering. "I— I hardly knew you, Solo. What has happened to you?"

"I suppose I am a changed man." Scott's quiet voice seemed almost rational. "What happened is that I learned something. I learned the message I bring to you."

"Whatever happened, it's great good luck you came along." Quamodian raised his voice to hide revulsion. "Molly says the Companions back on Earth don't believe in rogue stars . . ."

"They're right." The gray cowl nodded solemnly. "The rogues are a myth—that's something I learned." The gaunt man bent nearer, and Quamodian tried not to shrink from his breath. "Andy, the great thing I learned is that we human beings have always followed a false philosophy of life."

The words seemed commonplace, but Scott's hollow voice gave them a hypnotic power that Quamodian knew he would never forget.

"We tried to make competition the basic law of being. I guess we came to make that blunder because our forefathers had lived by hunting for too many million years, killing for survival. Anyhow, Andy, the rogue star is the mythic ideal of our killer kind. The perfect individual. Absolutely free. Omnipotent as anything. Immortal as the universe. Nothing anywhere can curb a rogue star."

"I know." Quamodian nodded uneasily. "That's why I'm afraid . . ."

"The rogue was once my own ideal." The gaunt man ignored the interruption. "Hawk's, too, I should imagine. When I came here to set up the stellar section, I was competing with everybody else in my field of science. I was a man and that was the game. I had to challenge the best brains from all the galaxies, gathered here at Exion. I had to beat the robots, all linked together in their transflex webs, sharing memory banks and programs that united them into a single monstrous mind. I had to match all the multiple citizens, pooling their logical processes as the robots did. I had to compete with all my fellow human beings who had given up their individual freedom for symbiotic union with the fusorians." The gray cowl tossed. "That was the rogue ideal, which pitted me against Cliff Hawk, and led me out to the runaway star he found."

"Solo, what happened there?"

"I found Hawk's so-called rogue." Scorn chilled the grating voice. "No rogue at all. A sentient sun— but born so far from all the galaxies that it had never encountered another intelligence. A feeble thing, ignorant and afraid. In flight from the whole universe. Its untrained mind was weaker than my own. It was afraid of me!"

He cackled into shrill laughter that bent him double and became a paroxysm of asthmatic wheezing. Quamodian caught his bony arm to steady him, and peered uncomfortably into his dark lair beyond the valve.

"That was my lesson," Scott gasped when he could speak. "I never came back to the stellar section, because I've learned a higher principle. The law of association. That's the law that drew the first cells of life together to begin the evolution of man. The same law the plants obey when they exhale oxygen for men to breathe, and the law we obey when we exhale carbon dioxide for them. That's the law that ties men into families and clans and nations. Andy, that's the same universal law that is now knitting men and fusorians and sentient stars into the symbiotic citizen called Cygnus."

"Maybe so," Quamodian muttered. "But what has this to do with my trip to Earth . . ."

"Forget the Earth." Scott's hoarse voice had become a croaking chant. "Forget Cliff Hawk and Molly Zaldivar. Forget all the false concerns of your misguided self and all the worthless goals you've been striving for. Forget the fool's law of competition. Try association."

Quamodian was edging warily backward.

"Listen, Andy." Scott's cold claws gripped his shoulder. "I've given up the rogue ideal. I'm telling the association story. That's my message for you. I beg you to join us in the universal fellowship of Cygnus."

Swept with a sudden panic, Quamodian twisted free. He retreated to the outer valve and stopped there, frowning, grasping for sanity. "I guess everybody has to make his own terms with society," he said at last. "But I don't want symbiosis. As a Companion of the Star, I'm a useful citizen. All I really need is Molly Zaldivar . . ."

His voice caught when he saw the gray claws on that thin gold blade. He dodged back to get a breath of clean air.

"Watch it, Scott!" he gasped. "Don't touch me."

"My touch is eternal life." Scott's flat, bright stare and his hollow voice held no trace of warmth or reason. "This syringe is loaded with symbiotic fusorians." His bloodless fist poised the glowing point. "A life-form older than our galaxy. Old enough to know the law of association. Flowing in your blood, the microscopic symbiotes will keep your body new. They'll mesh your mind with all of theirs, and with many billion human symbiotes, and with the sentient suns."

"Hold on, Scott!" Quamodian raised his empty hands and tried to calm his voice. "I can't quite imagine what you're up to. But I do know the citizen Cygnus—my own parents belong. I know that it allows no evangelism. People must ask to join. So I know you're somehow phony." He peered at the gaunt man. "If Molly didn't want you . . ."

23

"Let's forget our lonely selves," Scott was creaking. "Let's rejoice in everlasting union . . ."

As he spoke, the gold needle jabbed. Quamodian grabbed his sticklike wrist and felt a surge of metal force beneath the dirty robe. The needle quivered overhead, dripping yellow drops. Savage power forced it slowly downward.

Quamodian gasped for breath and caught a nauseating reek. He lunged for open air. The gray robe tripped him. Falling against the wall of the lock, he clung to that twisting stick, fought it off his throat.

"Forget the rogue!" Scott was wheezing. "Forget . . ."

His mad power died, and his rattling voice. The stick-wrist bent with a brittle crack. The lank frame slid down inside the dirty robe. Drops of gold fire spurted from the broken needle driven through the cowl.

Quamodian looked once, and staggered out into the icy wind. Hovering near, the flyer picked him up and carried him back to the edge of the ramp before the robot guardians arrived. He lay gratefully back in his seat for a long time, shivering in the flyer's warmth and gasping for good air, before he started asking questions.

"The guardians are unable to discover how Scott survived his encounter with the rogue star," the flyer informed him then. "They cannot determine how he got back to Exion Four, or why he landed here. But they report that he is dead."

"I guess—" Quamodian gulped uneasily. "I guess I killed him."

"The guardians observed the incident," the flyer

24

said. "They saw him fall against the hypodermic needle which pierced his throat and caused his death. They will file no charge against you."

"How could the needle kill him?" Quamodian asked. "If it contained benign fusorians?"

"But it didn't," the flyer said. "The luminescent fusorians in the syringe are not symbiotic. They are a related type, found in the reefs of space, which act as a virulent toxin in the blood of your species. The guardians infer that Scott came here to murder you."

"Why?" Quamodian shivered again. "Why me?"

"The guardians lack adequate files on the irrational patterns of self-destruction prevalent among your species," the flyer droned. "They can only answer your question with another. Who has any reason to stop your trip to Earth?"

"Cliff Hawk, perhaps." Quamodian scowled uncertainly. "I can't think of anybody else. But he's a good many galaxies away from here. The whole thing baffles me."

The flyer hummed for two seconds.

"The guardians will continue working on the case," it said. "They report many factors which still resist logical resolution. However, they do have advice for you, based on a first analysis of the available data."

"So?"

"If you return to your dwelling and remain inside, the computed probability of your premature termination is only point-o-two. If you continue your trip to Earth, however, the computed probability of an illicit termination of your life is point-eight-nine. The guardians advise you to go home."

25

"Thank the guardians," Quamodian said. "But Molly needs help." He sat up straighter. "Call the dome," he said. "Ask about my priority to Earth."

IV

The control dome reported that his priority request had been duly transmitted to Almalik, spokesman star for the citizen Cygnus. No priority had yet been issued.

"Be patient, sir," the flyer added sympathetically. "The sentient suns are hard to hurry. With life spans of many billion years, they have their own scale of time."

Quamodian grumbled and waited, watching the robot guardians remove the dead man and his rusted spacecraft. Comtemplating the computed probability of his own early termination, he grappled with the riddle of Solo Scott.

Scott's little sermon about association, taken by itself, made a weird kind of sense. Thinking back to his boyhood, Quamodian could see its truth in his own experience. The arrival of the fusorians on Earth had ended ages of competition and opened a new era of association. All his life, Quamodian had been torn between the two.

It struck him now that Scott was probably right. Self-interest may have been a necessary law of the jungle, but even the most primitive hunters had learned to work together. Competition had become a deadly sickness of higher civilization. The harshest therapy of the old Plan of Man couldn't cure it—not even with an explosive iron collar around the neck of every self-directed individual. When the fusorians came, most men welcomed them.

But Quamodian had elected not to join his parents in the new symbiotic union. Growing up in the disturbing transition years, he had come to love both ways of life. He yearned to keep his own individual freedom, however dangerous. But he also yearned, just as keenly, for the absolute security and peace the fusorians had brought.

With a sharp conflict of emotions, he had watched the end of man's old civilization. Sometimes sadly, he had seen almost every feature of it—religion and philosophy, politics and business, social custom and private habit—proved needless or silly or just plain wrong. Often approving, he had observed the end of war, of want, of man's old cruelty. He found that he loved both the old and the new too much to abandon either.

Forced to make his own decision when his parents accepted membership in Cygnus, he chose at first to compete. Struggling for academic marks, he won a Starscout scholarship that lifted him off the confused and crowded Earth into a more intense and complex existence in the transgalactic civilization—that must have been twenty years ago, if he converted universal time into the old solar periods.

In his own life, he reflected, the old jungle law had clearly gone wrong. Competing with robots and multiple beings and human symbiotes, he had failed his graduate finals. He had failed in a dozen pathetic

27

little business enterprises. Reaching Exion as a sort of experimental animal, he had failed to beat Cliff Hawk, failed to win Molly Zaldivar.

Only now, working with the Companions of the Star, had he found his own small but satisfying place in society. Not so final as the total self-surrender of symbiosis, it was still a useful social service. It was association enough for him—unless Molly changed her mind.

"Attention, sir." The flyer's drone broke into his brown introspection. "The control dome is calling us back to the ramp."

"Oh, sorry." Relieved, he gave instructions. The flyer swam back into the stream of traffic. A stalked horror of a citizen with members like bamboo shoots and a frond of brain tissue like a skirt around its waist had paused to let him move into the line of traffic on the ramp.

"Traffic control to Andreas Quamodian," the dome was flashing. "The multiple citizen Cygnus is fully qualified to issue priorities for intergalactic transist. Almalik, spokesman star for the citizen, has approved your application for a reservation number. You may enter the transflex cube."

Quamodian grumbled his thanks, and the flyer carried him toward the cube. The veteran of a good many intergalactic transits, he had never learned to enjoy them. The effects of transflection varied with the individual. Some felt nothing; a few reported pleasure or exhilaration. Most, to whom transit was unpleasant or terrifying, eased the strain of passage with drugs or hypnosis. Quamodian merely endured it.

Before they reached the cube, the flyer paused.

"Sir, the guardians are calling again. On the basis of a new analysis they have recomputed the probability of your early termination at point-nine-three. They still advise you to go home."

"Thank the guardians," Quamodian said. "Tell them I'm going on to Earth—and Molly Zaldivar."

"At least you are statistically safe until we reach our destination," the flyer assured him brightly. "A billion passengers arrive safe for only six who don't. Three of the six suffer nothing worse than dimensional rotation, with left sides exchanged for right. Two others undergo displacement of body tissue or prolonged psychosis. Only one passenger per billion is unaccountably lost. Even that one is statistically replaced. One passenger per billion is physically reduplicated through anomalous subspace refraction, so that the net loss is zero . . ."

"Shut up!" Quamodian growled. "I'm quite familiar with those statistics. As a monitor, I was once assigned to discover what becomes of that one lost passenger. I never solved the problem, and I prefer not to think about it now."

Sulkily silent, the flyer swam into the cube. Quamodian watched the diaphragm contract behind him, shutting out the endless file of waiting citizens. At once the flyer rocked and veered. Rotated out of space and time, routed by computation through a dozen or a hundred congruent folds of hyperspace, he felt as he always did: lost, stunned, and queasy.

The blue walls flickered and dissolved into a darkening, grayish haze. A queer roaring came hollowly from nowhere, swelling in his ears. Numbing cold drove through him, as if every tissue of his body had somehow been plunged into the dark zero of the space between galactic clusters.

Quamodian sweated and suffered. Transcience flight always did something to his location sense—researchers had experimented with the effect, but never explained it.

"Here we are, sir!" the flyer piped at last. "Was that so bad . . ."

Its cheery voice was cut abruptly off. It spun and pitched and fell. Quamodian saw streaks of blood-colored fire. He buried his wet face against his quivering knees and waited for his sense of place to adjust itself. It didn't. But after endless sickening seconds, he felt the flyer break out of that wild dive, and into level flight.

"Reporting trouble, sir," it whined. "Malfunction in all communication and navigation gear." It whirred and clicked and added blackly, "If somebody wished to keep us off the Earth, they have scored a point."

V

Quamodian raised his head and saw the sun. An unfamiliar star, blood-red and huge, too dull to hurt his eyes. It floated low in a dead-black sky, swelling across many degrees. Dark spots and streaks and convolutions covered its two enormous hemispheres, with almost the pattern of a naked human brain. Thick ropes of red plasma coiled away from both its polar coronas, brighter than its mottled face.

"It's sentient!" he whispered to the flyer. "I'm sure it's sentient. When neuroplasmic structures interfere with normal energy flow, a star gets that bloated look."

"No data," the flyer answered. "I'm scanning all my stellar files, but observable indices don't identify this star on my complete file of galactic charts. Possible inference: its location is outside the charted cluster."

With a spasmodic effort, Quamodian broke away from the hypnotic glare of that snake-wreathed star. He caught a rasping breath and glanced at the world beneath.

"It certainly—certainly isn't Earth." He gulped at a great lump of terror in his throat. "It looks like we were caught by that billionth chance!"

The flyer hung high above a flat and endless beach. To the north—or was it north—a vast sea lay flat and thick as blood beneath that dreadful sun. To the south—if that was really south—black cliffs rose above the level of the flyer.

That endless mountain wall was curiously sheer, curiously uniform, and curved very slightly toward the sea. Perhaps, he thought, it was an ancient crater rim, a thousand-mile bowl for that flat sea which seemed so dead that he wondered when its tides had ever worn its beaches smooth.

All around the twilight horizon, red auroras played. They writhed and coiled like blood-colored snakes, and struck their red reflections in the glassy sea. They sifted red fire beyond the walling peaks. With an unpleasant start, Quamodian found that he

31

could trace the star's plasma tentacles across that sullen sky, all the way from the polar coronas down to the little misty fingers reaching toward the beach, as if the sentient sun held sky and sea in a visible grasp.

"Lower," he told the flyer. "There's something on the sand I want to see."

Flakes of lighter color sprinkled the wide black beach, taking form as the flyer sank. Gray of weathered metal. Gleam of fading paint. White of naked bone. Dead citizens and their wrecked machines cluttered a three-mile circle of sand.

"I think we've found what becomes of those missing passengers," he said. "Call the guardians and file a report."

"Sir, I've been calling!" The flyer's shrill tone seemed deeply aggrieved. "I've been calling on all the transgalactic channels, with full emergency power. For some reason, I can't get a reply."

"Keep on calling. By the way—uh—how is our power supply?"

"Our emergency power pack is half depleted, sir," the flyer reported. "Shall we land to conserve it?"

"Not yet." He shaded his eyes against the cold red sun, to search that endless beach. "There! Toward the foot of the cliffs. Something I want to see. A little to the right. Those four queer towers. Land as close as you can."

The towers intrigued him. Spaced at the corners of a square, they were half crude masonry, built of unsmoothed-rocks laid together with clay. The higher halves were salvaged metal from the wrecks, welded crazily.

As the flyer settled, he discovered a web of cables

stretched between the towers: a skeleton cube, out-lined in taut bright wire; a second, smaller cube, suspended inside the first with tight wires which themselves outlined six tapered hexahedrons.

"A tesseract!" Wonder hushed his voice. "The essential circuitry of a transflex cube. What would that mean?"

"Relevant information unavailable. Data observ-able on this planet shows no logical relationship to any system or program of action in my files." The flyer hummed for three seconds and added sadly, "I'm sorry sir. I was not prepared for this."

"Keep trying," Quamodian said. "We've got to reach the Earth and Molly Zaldivar, in spite of—whatever it is!" He glanced at that surly sun and tried not to shiver. "How's the air?" he asked. "Fit for me?"

"Oxygen, thirty-point-seven-nine per cent," the flyer said. "Diluents, noble gases. Helium, neon, ar-gon. Temperature and pressure toward the lower limits of human tolerance. You won't like it, but it won't kill you."

"Thanks," he said. "Open—no, wait!"

An odd little procession came marching down the beach from a black round cave which he saw now above the rubble at the foot of the cliffs. Half a dozen tattered citizens. Three of them robots, badly damaged. Two yellow-crusted multipeds with miss-ing legs. A single human being, leading them all, waving a white rag on a stick.

The human was visibly a woman, in a faded garment made for a larger citizen of a very different race. Her thick dark hair had been clumsily haggled off, and black dirt splotched her visible skin.

Quamodian scrambled out of the flyer, ran a little way to meet her, and paused in wonder. Beneath the alien garb and the grime, she was not only beautifully human. In some way her loveliness was hauntingly familiar. He hailed her breathlessly, in old Earth English.

"Hello . . ."

"Stop!" She cut him off sharply, in the universal tongue. "Stand where you are. Identify yourself."

Her voice was brisk and cold, but something in its rich timbre reminded him—reminded him of Molly Zaldivar! That was what had teased his sense of recognition. The likeness sent a chilly prickling down his spine. Scrub off the dirt, replace her butchered hair, put her in human garb, feed her a few square meals, and she would be a dead ringer for Molly Zaldivar.

"I'm waiting." Sternly, she raised that tantalizing voice. "Let's have your standard identification code."

He made some vague, bewildered sound.

"Speak out!" She waved a signal, and the robots darted out around him. "I'm the authority here."

Stammering a little, he recited his universal identification pattern.

"Thank you, Monitor Quamodian." She nodded briskly. "I am also with the Companions of the Star. Senior Monitor Clothilde Kwai Kwich." She stressed the *Senior*. "What's the date, outside?"

He gave her the universal date.

"Thank you, Monitor." Calculating, she made an appealing little frown that belonged to Molly Zaldivar. "That means I've been here five years—five years too long!"

She nodded at the bloated sun.

"Time's hard to follow here," she added. "Because the day and the year on this planet are the same. The sun never moves in the sky. We can't even count the local years, because we can see no stars for reference points."

Listening, Quamodian closed his eyes. Except for its brisk authority, her rich voice was altogether Molly's.

"Wake up!" she snapped. "How did you get here?"

"I was in transflection transit from Exion Four to Earth," Quamodian said. "With travel priority from Cygnus to answer a trouble call from a girl named Molly Zaldivar." He saw no change in her dark-smudged face when he spoke the name, but he couldn't help asking, "You don't happen to have a twin named Molly?"

"Certainly not. Don't waste my time with idle talk. Monitor, you'd better wake up! We're all facing unprecedented problems here. Every effort must be directed toward their solution. As your superior Companion, I'll require you to cooperate. My subordinates may now identify themselves."

Speaking in unison, the three robots intoned a voice pattern which identified them as traffic safety inspectors. Curiously, all three gave the same serial number. The two yellow-shelled multipeds spoke in turn, but they were both assistant traffic safety inspectors and their identification codes were identical.

"They arrived a year after I did," Clothilde Kwai Kwich explained. "I had been assigned to discover what becomes of the statistically small number of passengers lost in transflection transit. Their assignment was to find what became of me. They entered the headquarters terminal as a team of two—an inspector and his robot assistant. I had been in route to Exion Four, and that was their destination."

Staring at the three damaged robots and the two crippled multipeds, Quamodian felt cold breath on the back of his neck.

"You see what happened," she went on. "The inspector was duplicated in transit. The robot assistant was triplicated. What is even more confusing, their identities were switched. All the robots now have the minds and memories of the original inspector. The duplicated original inspector has the logical programs and the memory banks of the robot assistant. Finally, they were all dropped here."

Her brisk voice cracked. "And that—" For a moment, beneath her commanding self-assurance, he heard the quaver of naked terror. She stiffened at once, recovering herself. "Monitor Quamodian, that's the sort of problem we face here."

"What about you?" He couldn't stop that impetuous question. "Did you notice any change in yourself?"

She flushed and trembled. Familiar auburn lights glanced in her short dark hair as she turned to gaze along that endless beach. Abruptly she swung back, her chin lifted in a small gesture of anger that stirred his most painful recollections.

"I resent personal questions," her voice was strained and quivering. "If you want objective information—I have seen evidence of some slight physical anomalies, which I prefer not to discuss. Let's get on to questions of survival."

"Agreed," Quamodian said. "Can you explain how we got here?"

"We've been collecting facts and putting hypotheses together." Uncertainty seemed to slow her voice. "Of course you understand that any firm conclusions will have to wait for the full analysis of data that I still hope to make when we get back to headquarters —if we do get back."

She shrugged angrily in that grotesque garb, as if to free herself from clutching fear.

"I'll tell what our evidence suggests." She nodded toward the dark-mottled sun. "I think that's a rogue star. I think it is systematically tampering with transflection traffic. The dated documents in the oldest wrecks show that they were highjacked many centuries ago, but the rate of this activity seems to have increased recently—about the same time that Solomon Scott set up his stellar project on Exion Four to investigate rogue stars."

"So the rogues are watching us!" He shivered in spite of himself in the steady wind that blew across the black beach toward that sullen sun. "Has Solo Scott been here?"

"No," she said. "We've checked all the wrecks and made up a register. All except a few very early victims have been identified. There are a few humans on the list. None that could be Scott." She gave him a probing look of Molly's. "Why do you ask?"

As he showed her Molly's transfac tape and told her about his encounter with Scott, the multipeds began chittering at the robots in some language of their own. Clothilde Kwai Kwich paused to listen as the three robots squealed back in unison.

"We've seen a strange machine," she told Quamodian at last. "Half a dozen times. Flying fast and low, just off the beach, as if spying on us. The inspectors inform me that it appears to fit your description of Scott's damaged craft."

"What do you make of that?"

She waited for the robots to squeal and the multipeds to answer.

"Scott was attempting to reach the vicinity of a rogue star," she translated for Quamodian. "The inspectors suggest that this was his rogue, that it somehow captured him when he arrived, that it sent him back to Exion Four as a sort of slave machine."

"That might account for the change in him." Quamodian nodded. "But why did he try to kill me?"

The robots squeaked and the multipeds stridulated.

"They suggest that the rogue has a friendly interest in Cliff Hawk's experiments on Earth," said Clothilde Kwai Kwich. "They suggest that it does not intend to allow you to intervene."

"Molly wants me there," Quamodian muttered stubbornly. "I don't intend to stop."

"You have a nut to crack before you reach the Earth." The girl's hollow eyes held a faint sardonic glint. "Because our isolation here is complete. Nobody answers our signals. If this is really Cliff Hawk's rogue, we're somewhere out between the galactic clusters. Our register lists a good many thousand citizens who have been marooned here. Not one has ever got away."

VI

Quamodian frowned inquiringly at Clothilde Kwai Kwich and pointed at the wire web stretched between those four rough towers.

"Somebody meant to get away," he said. "Somebody was setting up a transflection terminal . . ."

"And there it stands." She shrugged disdainfully. "It was standing there when I arrived. The engineers who built it were already dead and forgotten then. Their names are not even on our register."

"I studied transcience engineering once." Quamodian neglected to add that he had muffed his finals. "That tesseract circuit looks like a good copy of the working model we put together in the lab." Eagerness took his breath. "Maybe—maybe I can finish it!"

"It's finished now," she said. "Ready to test."

"What's wrong?"

"We can't try it till we know where we are." She listened briefly to the squealing robots. "The inspector believes this star is Cliff Hawk's rogue. If so, we could estimate the distance to the Exion terminal precisely enough. But a distance setting is no use without direction, and we have no points of reference."

"I know—" Quamodian bit his tongue. "I used to know directions. I've got a sense of place. The trouble is, transflection flight disturbs it. Usually it comes back when I arrive. This time—" Unhappily, he shook his head. "This time it didn't."

A breathless quiet had frozen them all. The robots twanged when he paused, and the multipeds bleated. They closed in around him. The girl's hungry face was white.

"Monitor Quamodian, the inspector recalls a research report on your transcience sense. Some experimenters convinced themselves that you had an unexplained perception of hyperspatial congruities. Others apparently suspected you of fraud, conscious or not. If you do have such a sense, now's the time to use it."

"I'll try," he muttered. "But I still feel lost."

In a groping way, he tried. The effort sharpened his queasy giddiness. Cold sweat broke over him. The beach tipped until the black cliffs hung over his head. The furious sun ballooned and wheeled around him.

"No use!" he gasped weakly. "Actually, I don't know how to try. It's nothing I know how to do. It's either there or not."

The creaking robots crowded closer.

"Better try again!" snapped Clothilde Kwai Kwich. "Or perhaps you like it here!"

"Almalik!" Anger crackled in him. "Don't you think I want to reach Earth and Molly Zaldivar . . ."

Something happened as he spoke. The rocking beach leveled under foot. The red sun settled into place. And all his giddy confusion was gone. He knew precisely where he was.

"There's Exion." He pointed into the sky. "To the right of the sun. Just extend the equator half a diameter out. The galaxies are lower, just above the sea."

"Monitor, are you sure?"

Doubt began to gnaw at his new certainty.

"I think—" he hesitated miserably, "I think I'm right."

Clothilde Kwai Kwich and her robots withdrew into a huddle near the towers. The two multipeds stood alertly near, as if they expected him to run. The robots squeaked and the girl whispered and presently they all came back.

"Monitor Quamodian, we have discussed this situation. It raises grave new issues. We can't be certain that your claimed transcience sense will enable us to orient the terminal controls. Even if the terminal works, we can't be sure the rogue will let us leave. Under these circumstances, the inspector suggests that we allow you to make the first test transit. Are you willing?"

"Of course I'm willing." But it had not occurred to him that the rogue might intervene again. "What are the chances—?" Staring at that serpent-haired star, he failed to finish the question.

"My subordinates won't risk a prediction." She frowned like Molly. "They can't place the rogue in any normal pattern, even for sentient stars. Its power is unlimited. But its motives are incomprehensible. Its sheer intelligence is just about absolute. But its ignorance of other beings—especially of human beings—is nearly total. Its resulting behavior can be appallingly naive, or stunningly clever, or simply insane." She shrugged. "Who knows what to expect?"

Quamodian helped set the terminal controls,

which were in a cargo barge buried in the black sand beneath the towers. Clothilde Kwai Kwich gave him a brisk handclasp. He walked back to his waiting flyer and waited for her signal.

She waved her hand. The flyer swam between the entrance towers, into that web of shining wire. He glanced toward that ominous sun, but it had already flickered and dissolved. He was lost again.

Gray spaces, roared around him and probing cold sucked away his life. The flyer rocked and spun until he thought the mad rogue had flung them into some more dreadful trap . . .

But then the careening flyer steadied under him. "Prepare to emerge, Mr. Quamodian," it sang in his ear, and the roaring storm of sound and sensation died away.

The skeleton walls of the wire tesseract had turned real around him. They were greenish-gray, and painted in bold black characters that identified the Wolf Creek Station on Earth. Ahead of him the exit gate expanded.

He felt stunned. The contrast was nearly too much for him. There was no alien beach, no red sea, no snake-armed rogue. Neither was there a bitter oxy-helium wind whipping at a long line of impatient citizens bent on business, competing for priorities and snarling at delay. In this pastoral quiet, Exion Four and the world of the rogue became twin nightmares that he didn't want to think about.

Quamodian leaned forward eagerly as the flyer glided out of the cube, and looked for the first time in his adult life on the warm, broad acres that were lit by the single sun of Earth.

Twenty minutes later most of his relief and all

Earth's pastoral charm had evaporated. He was snapping furiously at his flyer. "What do you mean, you can't reach Miss Zaldivar? I've come all this way from Exion Four. Do you mean I can't get a message to her now?"

"Your messages can't be delivered at this time, Mr. Quamodian. Your communication circuits are blocked."

"Nonsense! Try the local office of the Companions of the Star . . ."

"Also blocked, Mr. Quamodian. A local custom. I have been informed that in fourteen hours, local time, all the normal lines of communication will be open for service. But until that time . . ."

"I've no time for fools!" Quamodian shouted. "I've gone through a lot to get here, and I don't propose to twiddle my thumbs while these yokels divert themselves. Here, I'll go to that office myself!"

"Certainly, Mr. Quamodian." The flyer began to settle toward a dusty plaza in front of the transflex tower. "Of course," it added apologetically, "you will have to go on foot. By local custom, flyers are not permitted to operate more than one hundred meters from the transflex center at this time."

"Great Almalik! Oh, very well." Fussily Quamodian collected himself and stamped out of the opening door. "Which way?"

A voice by his ear answered, as the flyer activated its external speakers. "Down this street, Mr. Quamodian. The gold building with the ensign of the Companions."

He turned and stared. Behind him, the flyer quietly rose, drifted back to the tall, tapered, black transflex tower and settled to wait at its base. Quamodian was alone on the planet of his birth.

He was, he realized, more alone than he had expected. He knew that parts of Earth were still scarcely populated—nothing like the teeming metropolises of the hub-worlds of the universe: nothing, even, like the relatively minor planets of his university training and recent practical experience.

But he had not expected Earth, even this part of Earth, to be *empty*.

Yet there was not a soul in sight. He peered back toward the transflex tower: his waiting flyer, motionless and peaceful; nothing else. He looked down a long artificial stone boulevard: a school building, a hospital, a few supply centers—and no one in sight. He saw a park with benches and a playground, but no one was near any of them; saw parked vehicles, seemingly abandoned, a library without readers, a fountain with no one to watch its play.

"Ridiculous," he grumbled, and walked toward the building that glinted in the sun.

Earth's single star was hot, and the full gravity of his home planet was more than Andreas Quamodian had been used to for a good many years. It was a tiring walk. But there was something pleasant about it, about the dusty smell of the hot pavement and the luminous young green leaves of the trees that overhung the walk. Peace lay over the village, like a benediction of Almalik.

But Quamodian had not come to Earth in search of peace. He increased his stride, and chugged up the walkway, beside the flagpole that bore the standard of the Companions of the Star: the thirteen colored stars of Almalik in the dotted ellipses of their intricate orbits, against a black field of space.

The door did not open for him. Quamodian nearly ran into it; he stopped only just in time.

"What the devil's the matter here?" he demanded, more surprised than angry—at least at first. "I am Andreas Quamodian, a monitor of the Companions of the Star. Admit me at once!"

But the bright crystal panel did not move. "Good morning, Citizen Quamodian," said a recorded robot voice. "The Wisdom Creek post of the Companions of the Star is closed today, in observance of local religious custom. It will be open as usual on Monday."

"I'll report this!" Quamodian cried. "Mark my words! I'll call the Regional Office of the Companions of the Star . . ."

"A public communications instrument is just to your left, Citizen Quamodian," the robot voice said politely. "It is cleared for emergency use even on Starday."

"Emergency, eh? You bet it's an emergency." But Quamodian had had enough of arguing with recorded voices. He stalked along the flank of the gold-colored ceramic building to the communications booth, angrily dialed the code for the Regional Office—and found himself talking to another recorded voice.

"Companions of the Star, Third Octant Office," it said briskly.

"Oh, confound—never mind. Listen. I am Monitor Quamodian. I am in Wisdom Creek to investigate a reported emergency, and I find the local office closed. This lax operation is highly irregular! I demand the office be opened and . . ."

"Monitor Quamodian," reproved the robot voice, "that is impossible. Under our revised covenant with the Visitants, no local posts operate on Stardays so that local personnel may be free to engage in voluntary religious activities. Even Regional Offices are machine-operated during this . . ."

"But this is an emergency! Can't you understand?"

"Monitor Quamodian, my sensors detect no emergency situation in Wisdom Creek."

"That's what I'm here for! I—well, I don't know the exact nature of the emergency, but I require immediate assistance . . ."

"Our Wisdom Creek post will open promptly at midnight, local time," the voice informed him blandly. "Competent assistance will be available then."

"Midnight will be too . . ."

But the line clicked, buzzed and settled to a steady hum.

Muttering with anger, Quamodian tried Molly Zaldivar's code. But his flyer had been right; there was no answer.

Puffing with irritation as much as fatigue, Quamodian lowered himself to the steps of the office of the Companions and scowled at the empty street. How many millions of light-years had he spanned to be here, on this day, in this backwash of life? What tremendous forces had he enlisted to hurl him across the gulfs of space, to race against the dreadful fears that Molly Zaldivar's message had conjured up?

He licked dry lips and wiped perspiration from his

brow. He was a hero, ready to rescue maiden, towns-people, world itself. But none of them appeared to want to be rescued.

VII

Twenty-five miles southwest of Wisdom Creek, Molly Zaldivar did want to be rescued. At that moment she wanted it very badly.

Her old blue electric car had whined up the rocky mountain road, three thousand feet above the plain; below her she saw the flat, dry valley with the little town of Wisdom Creek huddled around the twin spires of the Transflex tower and the church. But now the road went no farther. It dipped, circled a spur of the mountainside, and went tumbling into the other valley beyond. From here on she would have to walk . . .

But that she could not do.

Above her she heard the restless, singing rustle of the creature Cliff Hawk called a sleeth. She could not see it. But she could imagine it there, tall as a horse but far more massive, black as space and sleek as her own hair. And she knew that at that moment she was closer to death than she had ever been before.

She tiptoed silently back to the car, eyes on the rocks over her head. The singing sound of the crea-ture faded away and returned, faded away and came back again. Perhaps it had not detected her. But it might at any moment, and then . . .

Molly entered the car and closed the door gently, not latching it. Breathing heavily—partly from nerves, partly from the thin, high air around her— she picked up her communicator and whispered, "Cliff? Will you answer me, Cliff, please?"

There was no sound except for the faint rustle of the sleeth, and the even fainter whisper of wind around the mountaintop.

Molly bit her lip and glanced over her shoulder. She dared not start the car's motor. It was not very loud, but the sleeth was far too close; it was a wonder it hadn't heard her coming up the trail. But the road sloped sharply away behind her. If she released the brakes the old car would roll on its out-of-date wheels; it would rattle and creak, but not at low speeds, not at first. And Cliff had told her that the sleeth would not wander more than a few hundred yards from the cave mouth. She was very close now, but the car would roll out of range in not much more than a minute . . .

And then what? Cliff did not answer. She *had* to see him—had to stop whatever he was doing, teamed with the rude, hard man who owned the sleeth. She would never be any closer than this, and what hope was there that the sleeth would be elsewhere if she tried again another time anyway?

"Oh, please, Cliff," she whispered to the communicator, "it's Molly and I've *got* to talk to you. . . ."

There was a rattle of pebbles and dust, and Molly craned her neck to look upward in sudden terror.

There was the sleeth, eyes huge as a man's head,

green as the light from a radium-dial watch. It was perched over her, the bright, broad eyes staring blindly across the valley. It was graceful as a cat, but curiously awkward as it floated in its transflection field, clutching at the rubble with claws that were meant for killing.

It did not seem to have seen her. Yet.

Molly froze, her ears tuned to the singing rustle of the sleeth. Its huge muscles worked supply under the fine-scaled skin, and the eyes slowly turned from horizon to horizon. Then it drifted idly back behind the rock, and Molly dared to breathe again. "Oh, Cliff," she whispered, but only to herself. She could not bring herself to speak even in an undertone to the communicator.

But even terror fades; the monkey mind of a human being will not stay attuned even to the imminent threat of death. Molly became aware of her cramped position on the scarred plastic seat of the car, cautiously straightened her legs and sat up.

If only Cliff Hawk would hear her message and come.

If only the sleeth would drift over to the other side of the mountain, give her a chance to make a mad dash for the cave mouth and the men inside.

If only—she was stretching for impossibles now, she knew—if only poor Andy Quam would respond to her plea for help, and come charging out of the transflex tower with weapons, and wisdom, and the strength to do whatever had to be done to stop Cliff from going through with this dreadful work . . .

But they were all equally impossible. Cliff couldn't hear her, the sleeth wouldn't go away. And as for Andy Quam . . .

Even in her fear she couldn't help smiling. Poor old Andy, sober and serious, loving and stuffy, full of small rages and great kindnesses ... of all the rescuing heroes a girl might imagine, surely he was the most unlikely.

The singing sound of the sleeth grew louder again, and fearfully she looked upward. But it did not appear.

Even the Reefer would be welcome now, she thought—that gaunt yellow-bearded giant who was Cliff Hawk's ally in his folly. She was afraid of the Reefer. He seemed like a throwback to a monstrous age of rage and rapine, a Vandal plundering a peaceful town, a Mau-Mau massacring sleeping children. He had always been polite enough to her, of course, but there was something about him that threatened devastation. Not that any additional threats were necessary. What Cliff was doing was bad enough in itself! Creating sentient life at the atomic level—trying to breed living, thinking tissue of the same stuff that was at the core of the sapient stars themselves. And worst of all, trying to duplicate in the laboratory the kind of life that made some stars rogues, pitted them against their fellows in a giant struggle of hurled energies and destroying bolts of matter.

She grinned suddenly, thinking again of Andy Quam: imagine pitting him against the Reefer! Why, he ...

Molly Zaldivar sat bolt upright.

She had just realized that the singing sound of the sleeth was gone. The only noise on the mountain was the distant, moaning wind.

She waited for a long moment, gathering her courage, then slipped quietly from the seat. She stood beside the vehicle, ready to leap back inside and flee, however useless that would be—but the sleeth was still out of range.

Carefully, quietly she took a step up the rock path, then another. A pebble spun and grated under her feet. She paused, heart pounding—but there was no response.

Another step—and another . . .

She was at the top of the path now. To her right the cave mouth waited, rimmed with crystal, a rubble of junked laboratory equipment in front of it. No one was in sight. Not even—*especially* not—the sleeth.

Molly broke into a trot and hurried toward the cave mouth.

At that moment the sleeth appeared, rocketing over the crest of the mountain, coming down directly toward her like a thrown spear. She could see its great blind eyes staring directly into hers; it was moving at sonic velocities, hundreds of miles an hour; it would be on her in a second. *"Cliff!"* she shrieked, and flung herself toward the cave mouth.

She never reached it.

From inside the cave a great puff of black smoke came hurtling out in a perfect vortex ring. The concussion caught her and lifted her off her feet, threw her bruisingly to the ground. The sound followed a moment later and was deafening, but by then Molly was past caring; explosion, painful skin lacerations, raging sleeth, all blended together in a slow fading of sensation, and she was unconscious.

What was real and what was dream? Molly

opened her eyes dizzily and saw the gaunt, bleeding face of Cliff Hawk staring down at her, aghast. She closed them again, and someone—someone, something, some voice—was calling to her, and she saw Someone trapped and raging, commanding her to come . . .

"Wake up! Confound you, Molly!"

"I'm awake, dearest," she said, and opened her eyes. It was Cliff. "We've got to get him out of there," she said earnestly. "He's lost and trapped and . . ."

"Who? What are you talking about?"

She caught her head in her hands, suddenly aware of how much it hurt. "Why—" she looked up at Cliff Hawk, puzzled. "I forget."

He grimaced. "You're confused," he announced. "And a pest, besides. What are you doing here?"

"I wanted to stop you," she said dizzily. She was trying to remember what the very important thing was that Someone had said to her in her dream. If it had been a dream.

"Thought so. And look what you've done! As if I didn't have enough trouble."

Molly abandoned the fugitive memory. "There was an explosion," she said. "I got hurt."

Cliff Hawk looked suddenly less angry, more worried. Clearly Molly was telling him nothing he didn't already know. The rivulet of blood that ran down from a scrape on his forehead divided around his nose, blurred itself in the blue stubble of beard on his cheeks and chin. It made him look like a dangerous clown. But a clown with some great fear riding his back.

"We—we had an accident. Molly, go back to Wisdom Creek."

She shook her head, and then, without preamble, began to cry.

Hawk swore violently, but his touch was gentle as he reached swiftly down, caught her shoulders, helped her to her feet and into the cave. Molly let herself weep without shame, but it did not keep her from seeing that the cave was in fact a workshop, lined with glittering metal, rich with instruments and machines. A corona of pale violet hung over a humming golden globe, now soiled and dented from whatever it was that had exploded nearby. She heard the distant howl of a power tube, screaming to itself like the bass-C pipe of a steam calliope as it sucked energy from the air. She let him find her a seat on a wobbly laboratory stool, accepted a tissue and dabbed at her nose.

"You've got to go back," Cliff Hawk told her with rough tenderness. "I'm busy."

"You're in trouble!" she corrected. "It's dangerous, Cliff. Leave the rogue stars alone! I'll go back to Wisdom Creek if you come with me."

"I can't. We've had this out before."

"But you're risking your life—the whole world . . ."

"Molly." Awkwardly he touched her shoulder. "I can't stop. Even if it costs me my life. Even if it destroys the world. Did you mean it when you said you loved me? Then go back and leave me alone."

VIII

Andy Quam puffed around the corner and shouted, "Say, there! Wait a minute, will you?"

The three boys he had spied were ambling down the dusty road, yards away. They paused and looked around at him, politely curious. "Morning, preacher," nodded one of them. "Help you?"

"Yes. I hope so, anyway. I mean—well, where *is* everybody?"

"Starday, preacher. All off worshipping, mostly. 'Cept us."

"I'm not a preacher, young man. I . . ."

The boy looked him over. "Then why do you wear that funny suit?"

Quamodian blushed. "It's the uniform of the Companions of the Star. I'm Monitor Quamodian. I'm trying to find . . ."

"Gee, preacher!" The boy was showing the first real signs of interest now. "Companion of the Star? Then you go all over the galaxies, honest? And see all the funny Citizens with the green skins and the two heads and . . ."

"It is very impolite to make fun of a Citizen's appearance," said Andy Quam severely. "We are all equally star-shared."

"Oh, sure. Gee! Ever seen a sun go nova, preacher? Or fought ammonia creatures on a gas giant, or . . ."

Andy Quam said honestly, "Young man, my task has been mostly supervisory and statistical. I have had no adventures of any kind. Except this one."

"You're having an adventure *now?*"

"More adventure than I like. There's something very serious going on. I'm looking for Molly Zaldivar."

The second boy, a chubby redhead, spoke up. "Gone to the hills, preacher. Looking for her friends, I bet."

"Shut up, Rufe! They're not her friends!"

"Who are you telling to shut up, Rob? Just cause you're soft on Molly Zaldivar . . ."

"I'm warning you, Rufe!"

"What's the secret? Everybody knows you're stuck on her. And everybody knows she likes that fellow that lives in the—get your hands off me!"

Andy Quam grabbed them hastily. "Boys! If you're going to fight, please wait till I'm finished with you. Did you say you know where Molly is?"

The redhead broke free and brushed himself off, glowering at the other boy. "About thirty miles from here. Bet she is, anyway. Gone to the cave where the fellow lives with the Reefer and that animal. Kill themselves one day, my father says."

"How do I get there?" Andy Quam demanded.

"Why—no way, preacher. Not on Starday. Unless you want to walk."

"But it's very important—" Quamodian stopped himself. The boy was probably right. Still, it was already late afternoon, local time on this part of the planet, and at midnight he would be able to get things straightened out. He said, "What's a Reefer?"

"Man from the reefs of space, of course. Got one of those reef animals with him. They call it a sleeth."

"Big one," the third boy said suddenly. "My brother claims it can kill you soon's look at you."

"Killed three hunting dogs already," confirmed Rufe. "I wouldn't go near it for anything," he added virtuously. "My father told me not to."

Andy Quam looked at him thoughtfully. He said, "I bet you can tell me how to get there, though."

"Might, preacher."

"You could even show me, if you wanted to."

"Get in trouble with my dad if I did."

"Uh-huh. Say, boys. Back in my flyer I've got some rare goodies from a planet in Galaxy 5. Care to try them? Then maybe you can tell me a little more about this cave up in the hills."

The boys clamored for a ride in the flyer. The hundred-meter limitation was still in effect, but Andy Quam shepherded them all inside, closed the doors and ordered the flyer to rise to its legal limit and hover. It was the best he could do for them. And good enough, to judge from their shouts and yells as they thrust each other out of the way to see from the ports.

For that matter, Andy was interested too. Apart from his burning anxiety to find Molly Zaldivar as quickly as possible, this was old Earth, home of Man.

He felt a vague disappointment as he looked from the hovering flyer. He had expected vast, fantastic ancient cities, or at least the fabulous monuments and ruins of the long human past. But there was nothing like that. The land that sloped away from Wisdom Creek was reddish-brown and empty. The village itself was a disappointment. Only the Star church looked striking from the air, star-shaped, five pointed wings projecting from its central dome. The roofs and columns of the wings were all a dazzling white, the dome itself black as space and transparent, with brilliant images of the thirteen component suns of Almalik swimming within it.

"That's my house there, preacher," cried Rufus. "And see that road? Goes out to the mountains. That's where Miss Zaldivar is."

Andy Quamodian leaned forward, over their heads, and peered into the distance. The village was cradled in the bend of a stream. To the south a dam across the stream made a long, narrow lake, crossed by a trestle that carried a road toward the high, hazed hills on the horizon. "That's thirty miles, you said?"

"Nearer twenty-five, preacher."

"Which hill is it?"

"Can't tell from here. Have to show you. Can't show you today, not till the Peace of Starday's over."

Quamodian looked at him sharply. The boy's tone was—what? Cynical? Merely disinterested? "How come you're not in church?" he asked tardily.

The boy's face was impassive. "We don't cotton to the Star," he said. "My dad says the old religion's good enough for us."

"But Almalik's not opposed to any other religion, boys. It's not mystical. It's—oh, you must have been taught all this! It's a symbiotic association of stars and men and robots and fusorians, that's all."

"Course, preacher," the boy said politely. "You mentioned goodies?"

Andy Quam wanted to say more, but restrained himself. As a Monitor of the Companions of the Star he had been well drilled in the basic principles of the symbiosis, but as a matter of fact, he realized, he had never heard them questioned before. In Galaxy 5, in the far worlds where most citizens were nonhuman and had no interest at all in his views, in school where everyone nominally, at least, shared the same services on Starday, even among the dedicated scientists of Exion Four, there had been either no dissent or no interest at all. Perhaps he'd got a bit rusty.

But he hadn't thought, not for one second had anything in his experience prepared him to think, that here on the birthplace of the human race there would still be opposition to the Star! No wonder Molly Zaldivar had had to send for him for help. If these boys were representative, Earth had no interest in the wide universe outside.

While the boys were munching the treats the flyer had produced from its stores, transparent green jellies that pulsed warmly as they were chewed and filled the mind with a thrilling montage of synthetic sensation, Andy Quam said diffidently, "But not everybody's like you, are they? I mean, Molly Zaldivar's in the Church of the Star. And so must others be, to justify that church over there."

"Oh, there's plenty branded cattle of the Star," Rufe said chattily, pulling a bit of jelly from between his teeth. "That's what my dad calls them. But Miss

Zaldivar doesn't go much. Sometimes she teaches Starday school, but not lately, far as I know."

"Anyway, that church is pretty old," said the tallest boy. "I expect it had a lot more people years ago. And besides—sweet Almalik!" he cried. "Look there!"

The first thing Andy Quam thought was that the boy had evidently had more to do with the Church of the Star than his father really approved of, using the name of Almalik to ease his emotions. The second thing was that that didn't matter. The boy's face was suddenly stark and afraid. Quamodian whirled, to face where the boy was pointing.

And then he saw it, something that violated the sweet peace of that Starday afternoon. He saw a great rope of fire, which seemed to extend from the blinding red disk of the setting sun—which had a sudden dreadful resemblance to Cliff Hawk's rogue. He saw it coiling like a monstrous snake of fire in that serene blue sky, thrusting savagely down through the white tufts of cumulus that drifted toward the mountains.

"Preacher!" cried Rufe, scared. "What is it?"

But Quamodian did not know. It looked almost like the plasma effector of some transcience intellect, except that it was too enormous, its white blaze too painfully bright.

Like a snake of fire attacking from the sky it coiled and struck, recoiled and struck again, recoiled and struck three times into those low, far hills. Then it withdrew, sucked back into the setting sun.

A thin column of dark smoke rose from the shallow gap where it had struck. Presently an immense dull booming, like far thunder, rumbled out of the sky. The vast deep sound rolled away, leaving the valley bathed again in the sunlight of the serene Starday afternoon.

"Preacher, what was it?" demanded one of the boys, but Andy Quamodian could only shake his head. Then his eyes widened, his jaw dropped.

"Those hills!" he cried. "Isn't that where you said . . ."

"Yes, preacher," whispered the boy. "That's where the cave is. Where Molly Zaldivar is right now."

IX

That distant voice was still whispering to Molly, though she couldn't quite hear it, couldn't quite make out what it said or who it was that spoke. But it was a terribly *pained* voice, the sound of a mind in rage and agony.

Cliff Hawk kept talking to her, demanding that she leave, harsh, even threatening, warning her that there was danger here. "Of course there's danger," she cried suddenly. "Why do you think I came? I want you to stop!"

He sighed and looked at her. His face, she saw, was terribly lined. Young, strong, quick, he had come in the last few weeks to look unendurably old.

"You want me to stop, and you don't even know what I'm doing," he said.

"You can remedy that."

He looked away. After a moment he turned to the violet-lighted globe and studied it, still not speaking. Then he said, "We're searching for intelligence. For minds anywhere not in transcience contact with intergalactic society. The Reefer and I have built our own equipment—very sensitive equipment. One contact turned out to be the hysterical mind of a small human boy, lost in the wilderness of a new planet out in Galaxy 9. But the strangest contacts are the rogue stars . . ."

"What's a rogue star?"

He probed at the dried blood beside his nose, thoughtfully. "Solitary sentient stars," he said. "They don't belong to the civilized community. Most of those we've picked up—all of them, maybe—are at enormous distances outside our own galactic cluster. Yet somehow—" he hesitated, shrugged. "I don't know why. Most of them seem angered or alarmed when they sense us. But there's one, out beyond Exion—" He stopped.

Molly Zaldivar shuddered. She tried to remember something, but it was outside the reach of her mind.

Cliff Hawk was lecturing now, his eyes fastened on limitless space. "Thinking machines are all alike. Whether they are human brains or fusorian committees or sentient stars or computing robots, they all possess certain features in common. All thinking things have inputs—from sensory organs or tape readers or sensitive plasmas. They all have data storage units—magnetic cores or neurone cells or spinning electrons. They all have logic and decision units—synaptic or electronic or transcience patterns.

They all have outputs—through motor organs or servo machines or plasma effectors."

He stopped thoughfully, seeming to listen to the drone of energy fields and the distant scream of the power tube.

"Go on, dear. How do you tell a rogue star from a lost boy?"

Cliff Hawk hesitated, as though trying to relate the girl's presence to what he was talking about, but she urged him on with a gesture. "Our steady state universe is infinite," he said. "Truly infinite. Endless. Not only in space and time, but also in multiplicity." The worry and resentment faded from his worn face as the theory absorbed him. "The exploding galaxies called quasars were the first proof of that—galactic explosions, resulting from extreme concentrations of mass. Space is distorted into a curved pocket around a dense contracting galactic core. When the dense mass becomes great enough, the pocket closes itself, separating from our space-time continuum."

He was in full flight now. Molly heard a distant sighing, remembered the sleeth and shivered. Was that fearsome creature still lurking about? But she did not dare interrupt him.

"The visible quasar explosion," he droned on, "results from the sudden expansion of the remaining shell of the galaxy, when it is released from the gravitation of the lost core. Each lost core, cut off from any ordinary space-time contact with the mother galaxy, becomes a new four-dimensional universe, expanding by the continuous creation of mass and space until its own maturing galaxies begin shrinking past the gravitational limit, budding more new universes."

From the cave mouth blood-colored dusk seeped in, mingling with the violet hues of the aurora. It was growing hard to see. Molly stirred restlessly, stifling a sigh.

"But the rogue stars," said Cliff Hawk, "are in our universe. Or we think they are. Or . . ."

"Or you're talking too much," rumbled a new voice, and Molly Zaldivar spun around to see a great bear of a man, wearing a dirty yellow beard, peering in at them from the cave mouth. In the red gloom he looked menacing. But far more menacing still was the great, restless bulk of the creature beside him. The sleeth.

Cliff Hawk blinked and returned to reality. For a moment his gaze brushed Molly Zaldivar as though he had forgotten she was there and was astonished to find her. But then his whole thought was concentrated on the man at the cave mouth.

"Reefer! What's the word? How bad is the damage?"

The Reefer opened a soundless grin between dingy yellow mustache and grimed yellow beard. "Bad enough," he said. "But we're still in business. What happened?"

"I— I—" Hawk glanced again at Molly Zaldivar. "I was just checking in the cave when I heard Molly groaning, and I . . ."

"And you forgot everything else and went to her. Ah, that's to be understood. A pretty face is more than a star to you, of course."

Hawk shook his head. "I've been telling her to go away."

"Beyond doubt. That's why you're lecturing the

girl like a child at Starday school, eh?" He patted the great bulk of the sleeth. "We understand, do we not?"

Hawk gazed at the Reefer with mingled anger and apology, then turned to Molly. "I'm sorry," he said. "But the Reefer's right. You've got to go back to Wisdom Creek."

"No! Not until you tell me what you're doing here!"

"Girl, he's been telling you," rumbled the Reefer. "What do you think all those words were that he was pouring out at you when I came in? More than you need to know. More than you should know, I think."

"But nothing that made sense to me," Molly persisted. "How are you trying to communicate with rogue stars?"

The massive head shook with laughter. "Communicate with them, girl? Then maybe he didn't tell you, after all. It's not just communication we're after. We're building one of our own!"

Cliff Hawk broke the shocked silence that followed the Reefer's words: "That's the truth of it, Molly. Or close enough. We can't really communicate with the rogue stars, not directly. We've tried that a thousand times, and it's past our abilities. Solomon Scott tried to reach one. He never came back. But we can—we think we can—build a sort of mathematical model of one. An analogue. A small imitation, you might call it. And through that, here on Earth, we may be able to reach them, find out what we want to know."

"But that's dangerous!" protested Molly. "Aren't rogue stars terribly dangerous?"

The Reefer boomed, "Not a bit, girl! Look at our cave here—you can see there's no danger at all!" And his great laugh filled the cave, drowning out the distant whines and drones.

Cliff Hawk said uneasily, "In order to duplicate the structure of a rogue star we had to duplicate some of the environmental features. Not really. Not in degree. But we needed great pressure and temperature, and—well, as you can see, we had a little accident."

"Little enough," flashed Molly Zaldivar. "It nearly killed you—and me, for that matter!"

"That's why I want you to go back to Wisdom Creek, Molly. Right away, before . . ."

"Now stop that!" shouted Molly Zaldivar. "I won't go! I was afraid what you were doing was dangerous; that's why I sent for And—well, never mind! But now that I know it, I won't stop until I make you give it up!"

"Impossible. I'll take you back."

"You won't!"

"Great Almalik, girl!" shouted Cliff Hawk, his face showing animation again for the first time. "What's got into you? Don't you understand, I don't want you here! Why won't you go?"

"Because I love you, you idiot!" cried the girl, and broke into tears.

There was silence then, even the Reefer saying nothing, though his eyes winked comically under the bushy yellow brows and his bearded face grinned hugely at the spectacle.

They stood staring at each other, Molly Zaldivar

and the man she loved. The silence protracted itself.

And then Molly shivered. "Something's—wrong," she whispered. "I'm scared, Cliff."

Cliff Hawk's stern face lifted. He stood listening, to something that he could not quite hear.

In the opening of the cave mouth the sleeth moved restlessly, the shimmer of its transflection field rippling light across its night-black hide. The Reefer stared at it, then away.

"Girl," he rumbled, "you're right about that. The sleeth's spooked. You know what I think? I think we've got a visitor."

X

Deep under the cave lay a tunnel, driven into the mountain by ancient prospectors a millennium earlier, beaded with galleries thrusting out from the main shaft to seek for gold or silver ores that were never found. For ten centuries they had lain empty, until Cliff Hawk and the Reefer came to fill them with their machines and instruments, to use them to hatch a new life that would serve as their contact with the rogue stars.

In one of these galleries, in a vault that the men had enlarged and bound about with steel and transflection energies, there was a region of great pressure and heat. All the energies of the screaming power tubes were funneled to keep that hot, dense plasma alive. It was an incubator, designed to produce a new life.

And it had succeeded.

Down there in the hot, crushing dark, Something stirred.

Its first knowledge was of pain. It had been born in a place where nothing like it had ever been before, a place that was innately hostile to all things like itself.

It stirred and reached out with an intangible probe of energy. The probe touched the energy-bound steel that kept its plasma environment intact, and recoiled.

I am caught, it told itself. I do not wish to be caught.

And then it fell to pondering the question of what it meant by "I." This occupied it for many thousands of microseconds—a long time in its life, which had just begun, but only a moment by the human standards of the, as yet unknown to it, world outside its pen. Overhead, Cliff Hawk was studying his instruments, ranging into galaxies millions of light-years away. The Reefer was roughly checking the tools and power tubes in the higher cave above, while his sleeth slipped silently and sightlessly around the crest of the hill. And down its slope Molly Zaldivar had just abandoned her old blue electrocar and was stealing toward the entrance.

At that point the new Something in the plasma field concluded its first serious deliberations with a conclusion worthy of a Descartes: I do not know what I am, but I know that I am something capable of finding out what I am.

And it proceeded experimentally to seek a further

solution. Gathering its energies, it thrust again at the metal energies that bound it; thrust hard, with neither thought of damage to itself (it had not yet learned the habit of self-preservation) nor interest in the consequences to its environment.

It thrust—and penetrated.

The dense, hot plasma burst free into the cave, shaking the entire hill, destroying its own gallery, melting down the steel bottle that had held it. As it broke free it died; the energies from the power tube that had replenished it were automatically cut off— which saved the hill, and half the countryside around, from destruction. Overhead, the tremor it caused shorted connections, started a fire, caused secondary explosions in a dozen places. It tossed Molly Zaldivar to the floor, rocketed a shard of metal across Cliff Hawk's brow, and threw the Reefer to his knees, where he shouted in anger and pain and called to his sleeth.

The thing that had been born in the plasma did not die. It registered this fact in its billion billion coded electrons without surprise. It had not been sure that it was alive, and had not feared to die. It hung in the corridor, while acrid chemical smoke and bright radiant heat whirled around it, untouched by them, hanging now in its own transflection forces, independent of its environment.

And free.

Now its probes could reach farther. They crept out onto the face of the mountain and lightly touched the unconscious mind of Molly Zaldivar, who moaned in fear and tried to open her eyes. They touched and penetrated the stark, bare thoughts of the sleeth. They studied Cliff Hawk and the Reefer, dismissed the inanimate rock and metal of the mountain and its caves, reached out toward the human minds in Wisdom Creek and found them not worth inspection, scanned the myriad men, women, children, bees, turtles, dolphins, dogs, apes, elephants of Earth and filed them for future examination, reached out to the moon and the planets, shaped themselves and stretched to touch the sun itself.

Briefly, lightly, its probes met another—the questing reach of another rogue mind, infinitely powerful, infinitely far away. Dimly, for half a nanosecond, it sensed the senses of that awed watcher . . .

All in the first few seconds of freedom.

Then they recoiled, and the thing that had been born so few moments before contracted in upon itself to think again. For some of the things it had touched had caused it certain sensations. It did not recognize what these sensations were, but it felt they were important. Some of them—those caused by the entity it had not learned to identify as Molly Zaldivar—were pleasant. Others—those caused by that larger, more distant entity it could not yet recognize as the sun—brought about sensations which it could not yet identify as fear. It needed time to study the meaning of all these things.

It contracted into itself and thought, for many microseconds.

Presently a probe stretched out from it once more. There were certain other elements in its environment which it had passed over in its first examination, about which it wanted more information.

It touched the "mind" of the sleeth again, but lingered for a moment, studying it. In this simple construction of cells and patterns it recognized something that might serve it. Yet there were even simpler patterns nearby. The thing reached out and looked at Molly's abandoned electrocar, at the great tracked handling machine that Cliff Hawk and the Reefer used for moving earth and heavy machines, at the instruments and machines of the cave themselves. It sensed another being, somehow more like itself but dim in infinite distance.

Hesitantly the probes returned to the thing down in the blazing gallery below.

It needed more time for thought. It wished to consider what it was that stirred within itself in regard to these things.

It had not yet learned to call these stirrings "hunger."

Cliff Hawk lifted his head from the hooded viewtubes of his instruments and shouted, "Reefer! You're right! There's something near us that wasn't here before!"

The Reefer nodded his great head slowly. "Thought so." His little dark eyes were hooded. "Question is, what?"

Molly Zaldivar struggled to her feet and caught at Cliff Hawk's arm. "Please stop, dearest! Don't go any farther. Let's call for help before it's too late."

Impatiently he shook her arm off, but she clung. "Cliff, please. I'm afraid. I felt something nearby before and it frightened me. Let me call Andy Quam and . . ."

He jerked his head around to glare at her. "Quamodian? Is he on Earth?"

"I—I think so, Cliff. I sent for him, because I was so worried."

Cliff Hawk laughed sharply. "Little Andy Quam? You thought he could help in *this?*" He shook his head, dismissing little Andy Quam, and turned to the Reefer. "Could we have hatched something? Were you inside the lower galleries?"

The Reefer shook his shaggy head. "Just passed by the mouth. The power tubes were running free, no load, and I had to adjust them. But there was something burning down there."

"Idiot!" snapped Cliff Hawk, and bent to turn a switch. A bank of viewers lighted up before him on the wall, revealing the entrance to the lower cave, a jumble of machinery, a blank rock face where a gallery ended—and nothing. Five of the viewers showed only the shifting whiteness of their scanning traces; no picture came through.

(Down in that lower cavern, hovering in the smoky fire where the burned-out cameras stared eyelessly at it, the thing that had come from the plasma tank completed its consideration and stretched out another probe. It was reaching for the sun. It had concluded that the danger in the sun needed action. The thing in the lower cavern massed perhaps an ounce and a half of stripped electrons and plasma. The mass of the sun was some 2×10^{33} grams, a third of a million times the planet Earth. The thing did not regard these odds as important.)

Molly Zaldivar shivered and moved away. Her bruises were beginning to trouble her now, and Cliff Hawk seemed to have forgotten she was alive; he and that terrible Reefer, with his face burned black and seamed with scars, were shouting at each other, pointing at the banks of instruments, acting in general like lunatics. Molly Zaldivar did not attempt to follow what they were talking about, except that something big had happened. But it could not be anything good; of that she was certain.

Her eyes widened. "Cliff!" she cried. "Listen!"

(The thing had acquired a great deal more skill in handling its functions in the past few thousand microseconds. While one probe was reaching out, invisibly and intangibly, to touch the Sun, it found itself able to mount other probes. One extended itself to touch those simplest of patterned creatures that it had discovered on the upper part of the mountain.)

"What's the matter, Molly?" Cliff was irritated, she knew; but she could not stop.

"Listen—outside! That's my car, starting up!"

And now all three of them could hear it, the distant tiny whine of the electrocar. They leaped for the cave mouth, all three of them, while the sleeth bobbed silently out of their way and stared. Before their eyes the little car started to move up the mountain toward them.

There was no one at the wheel.

The sleeth darted abruptly toward it, recoiled, and returned to the cave mouth like a hurled arrow. "Easy, girl!" shouted the Reefer, and turned to cry to Cliff Hawk, "The animal's caught a whiff of something. Careful! I can't control it when it's like this . . ."

But that danger dwindled into nothingness even before Molly Zaldivar realized what it was. For something more alarming happened and caught them all unawares.

Outside the reddening sunset brightened, flashed

into an explosion of white-hot brilliance. Something shook them, threw them against each other and the walls. The light dwindled and returned; dwindled again, and returned again, and on this third time struck with such violence that, for the second time that day, Molly Zaldivar found herself hurled into unconsciousness. As she fell into blackness she heard the Reefer shouting, "The star! Great Almalik, Hawk, we're being hit by the star!"

XI

Quamodian shivered. Leaning past the boys clustered at the window of his flyer, he shaded his eyes to study that thin column of dark smoke which rose straight above the shallow notch in the blue-hazed hills. The three boys moved closer to him, breathless and pale.

"Preacher, what did it hit?" the dark boy whispered suddenly. "Did it hurt anybody?"

"I don't know," said Andreas Quamodian. He groaned and slammed his fist against the unbreakable glass. "But I've got to find out!"

"The sun did it," said Rufe breathlessly. "I saw it. It hit the Reefer's place."

Absently, staring at the thin beacon of smoke, Andy Quam said, "Who's the Reefer?"

"A man from the reefs of space. He lives up on

73

Wolf Gap ridge—right where you see that smoke. Him and his sleeth."

Quam glanced blankly at the boy. "A sleeth?"

"It's a thing from space. It hunts. The Reefer trapped it when it was a cub. He raised it for a pet. My uncle says he rides it now, but I don't know. Cliff Hawk doesn't, I know that. Nobody would dare touch it but the Reefer."

"They were bred to hunt pyropods," said the smallest of the boys suddenly. "The sleeth can catch a pyropod and claw it to scrap metal."

Quam said harshly, "I don't care about the sleeth. Or the Reefer. What does Cliff Hawk have to do with all this?"

Rufe shrugged. "The Reefer brought him up. Brought his sick Mom here from the reefs before he was born, then sent him off to the stars to learn to be a transflection engineer. That's what my dad says."

"What else does your dad say about Hawk?"

"Says Hawk's building something for the Reefer. Contraband. Don't know what kind, but they smuggle in machines that humans aren't supposed to have without permission from the Star."

The smallest boy whined, "I want to go back down, preacher. I want to go to Starschool."

"Jay! You know we all said we weren't going to go . . ."

"Shut up, Rufe! I want to ask my Starschool teacher about the thing that hit the ridge. I'm scared, and Mark knows nearly everything. I want to see him!"

The redheaded boy looked at Andy Quam and shrugged. "Mark's a robot," he said. "But Jay's maybe right. Mark might know something."

Without thought Andy Quam's fingers reached out to the controls, but the flyer, listening, had anticipated his thought. They were already dropping to the ground.

"I'll take you there, Jay," said Andy Quam eagerly. "Provided you let me come along. I want to know too!"

They hurried up the graveled walk, under the multiple suns of Almalik imaged in the space-black dome of the church. The boy Jay guided Quamodian through hushed passages to Mark's schoolroom.

It was nearly empty, only a score or so brightly dressed children clustered at the front and a smaller, shabbier group lounging skeptically at the back. The robot paused to greet them.

"Come in, students. We are telling the wonderful story of the Visitants and the precious gifts they brought to the old human savages, centuries ago. Please take your seats."

The three boys slipped quietly into empty seats along a back bench, alongside the others who wore the worn and faded fiber clothing of the free people who have never accepted the Star. Quamodian walked past them, down the aisle to where the brighter garbed children of civilization sat on the front benches. He stopped and planted himself in front of the robot.

"Robot Inspector, I'm sorry to interrupt . . ."

The robot hung in the air before him, its tall black shining case reflecting the lights of the room and of its own oval of flame-bright plasma. The plasma flickered, darted half a yard toward him, flicked a dark, whiplike effector toward his face.

"Sir, you cannot interrupt," the robot intoned, its voice ringing like tossed pebbles against the low, blue dome.

"I can, Robot Inspector. I am your superior in the Companions of the Star. I am Monitor Andreas Quamodian."

"Even so, sir," pealed the robot, "you cannot control me today. Our new compact allows no official duties to interfere with voluntary religious activities on Starday. Teaching this class, Monitor Quamodian, is my voluntary religious activity."

Andy Quam stood his ground, disdaining the effector that tried to wave him away. "Robot, an emergency exists." He heard the ripple of excitement from the children and lowered his voice. "A very grave emergency, I'm afraid. Three plasma bolts from the sun have just struck near here. Human beings may have been injured, even killed."

Gently but firmly, the dark tip of the effector coiled around his arm, propelled him irresistibly toward the benches. "You must wait, sir," sang the robot as the staring children tittered. "Be seated. Be still. Be attentive, all of you, as I resume the wonderful story of the Visitants and their fusorian gifts to man."

Andy Quam muttered under his breath, but clearly it was no use. He stalked back down the aisle to the back benches, where Rufe gave him an approving grin. "You're okay, preacher! We don't like robots either."

"Hush, boy," said Andy Quam as severely as the robot. He sat glowering bleakly at the dark case of the robot, where its mark number was blazoned just under the bright-starred orbital pattern of Almalik.

Perhaps the robot was hard to manage today, but tomorrow would be different.

"The fusorians," sang the robot melodiously, retracting its effector and floating higher toward the blue dome, "are older than the stars, and all of them are very wonderful. They are microscopic creatures that live by fusing hydrogen atoms, and they evolved in space—so long ago that they have divided into many millions of different species. The reefs of space are built of atoms which some fusorians create. The Visitants are a special race of fusorians which live like symbiotes, inside the bodies of creatures like man."

"Bugs!" hissed the redheaded boy to Quamodian. "My dad says they're nothing but parasites!"

"In the wonderful partnership of man and fusorian," the robot trilled, "each benefits, neither is harmed. For the Visitants are wonderfully wise and just. They have evolved transcience intellectic patterns which knit their colonies together and link them all with the sentient stars. And so we are all united, all joined into the great multiple Citizen named Cygnus, whose spokesman star is Almalik."

"Slaved, you mean," whispered the redheaded boy.

"That is," sang the robot, its oval of plasma pulsing rhapsodically, "so are we joined if we accept the gift of the Visitants. On the great day when we join the Star they will jump in a fat golden spark to your skin. Their colonies will penetrate every cell of your body. They will destroy all marauders and all wild cells, and keep you young forever. They bring you utter happiness, and utter peace. This is the gift of the Visitants."

"Hogwash," the redhead muttered. "Preacher, why don't you make him shut up?"

"And here with us on this Starday," cried the singing voice of the robot, "we are fortunate, children, blessed by the Visitants. For we have with us a Monitor of the Companions of the Star!" Like lightning, a pale effector stabbed forth and burst in a shower of light over Andy Quam's head as the children turned and stared. "For great Almalik can only help us and guide us, he cannot fight for his own right cause. So we Companions fight for him, Monitor Andreas Quamodian here as well as, more humbly, my poor robot self."

Quam swallowed angrily, torn between the desire to stalk out of the room and the yearning to leap to his feet and denounce this willful robot who spoke of duty but would not help him in the emergency that had blasted the mountains.

"Of course," the robot added delicately, "Monitor Quamodian and I do not view all questions in the same light. Sometimes we differ. Sometimes, perhaps, one of us is wrong. But that too is just and proper, for the peace of the Star keeps us free, while joining us in rewarding fellowship."

It bobbed soundlessly for a moment, as though entranced with its own words, while its pale oval of plasma blushed briefly blue. "Now we are finished," it said at last. "Children, you may leave. Monitor Quamodian, I thank you for being with us today."

Andy Quam pushed furiously down the aisle, through the knots of chattering children, to confront the robot. "Robot Inspector," he cried, "How do you fight for Almalik when you won't even help me in this important matter?"

"Patience, Monitor Quamodian," purred the robot. "There are evil men and evil stars who reject the universal good of all. I join you gladly in fighting them, but under our compact Starday is . . ."

"Just another day!" Quamodian shouted roughly. "Rogue men are plotting with Rogue stars! There is great danger here, and it cannot wait on your convenience!"

The robot bobbed silently in its transflection field, as though it were considering what to do. Half-formed effectors budded around its case and were withdrawn; its plasma oval turned opalescent as pale colors chased themselves through it. It said at last, "The situation is grave, Monitor Quamodian."

"You don't begin to know how grave," Andy Quam said bitterly. "Didn't you hear me? Three bolts of plasma from the sun! That would have been impossible for any member of Cygnus without grave provocation. So there must have been provocation— something very dangerous, very serious, going on out in the hills!"

"We have recorded that phenomenon," the robot agreed melodiously. "It is more serious than you think, perhaps, Monitor Quamodian."

Quam brought up short. Had the robot heard from Senior Monitor Clothilde Kwai Kwich? "More serious than I think? What . . . ?"

"But nevertheless," the robot went on, "the compact is clear. You may not compel me today. And I advise—*we* advise, most urgently—that you undertake no action without our aid. You see, Monitor

Quamodian, we have recorded the presence of extreme hazards about which you know nothing."

Quamodian stuttered, "I d-d- I *demand* that information! Right now!"

"Under the compact—" sang the robot.

"Blast the compact!"

"Under the compact," the robot repeated serenely, "you may make no demands. I will do for you only what I wish to do freely, as part of my voluntary religious observance of Starday." It hesitated for only a second, while the shimmering colors on its plasma oval spun madly, then burst into a bright, almost golden fire. "Voluntarily," it sang, "I elect to aid you now. Will you mount on my back, Monitor Quamodian? I will convey you at once to the site of the sunbolts. For in truth there is danger; a rogue star has been born there, and lives and grows!"

XII

The thing had grown now, grown even while its effectors were reaching out to the sun and the sun's triple-stroked reply was coming back. It had passed Descartes' *Je pense, et puis je suis,* and that milestone surmounted, had put aside its examination of itself for examination of its world. *Dark. Alone. Particles.* It discovered that some of the particles were organized into macrostructures; it did not label these "matter," but it grasped at once that they operated as vector units, a myriad whirling charged bits contriving a mean motion exerting a mean force. *Warmth. Radiation.* Free of the heat of its exploded womb, it sought other energy sources, tapped them, used them, owned them.

I move, it "thought"—a true thought, joining together its sense of self and an operator; and it swam slowly along its deep tunnel, reaching for new sensation and new strength. *Pull. Gravity. Lift.* It slid through material obstacles or brushed them aside. Behind it lay a trail of erupted doors and demolished tiers of supplies. *Search. Search.* It gave a name to what it was doing, and the sense of a goal. Search for what? It sought that kindred mind and touched it again—infinitely far, yet jealously concerned.

It became aware of a kind of radiation that was itself structured, that possessed patterns that were neither random nor meaningless. *I?*

The thing paused, palping the faint currents of sensation that emanated from distant sources. *Affirmative. I. Not "I," but another "I."*

It had recognized that there were other creatures in its world, other competitors for energy or matter or space—or companions.

In the cavern above, Molly Zaldivar roused briefly from the stunned shock that held her, and moaned in terror. Something was studying her. Something that caused fear. Something utterly strange, that had never been in this world before.

XIII

Molly Zaldivar stirred and returned to consciousness. She lay across the crumpled legs of a laboratory stool, and one of them was stabbing her with its shattered end. The cave workshop was hissing, moaning, crackling with electrical shorts and hot, cooling metal. The pale violet corona that once had enshrouded a globe of gold now threw itself like a tattered net from point to point, dying and returning, hissing and crackling. There was smoke from somewhere outside the cave, a heavier, choking smoke from within.

She rubbed impatiently at her forehead, drew her hand away and saw, without surprise or fear, that it was bloody. But she was alive. She tried three times before she could speak.

"Cliff. Cliff, where are you?"

Hawk's voice answered at once, but weakly, more a whisper than his normal gruff tone. "I—I don't know exactly, Molly. Are you all right?"

She glanced down at herself—clothes a horror, skin bruised and cut, dirty and damp. But more or less functional, she decided. "I think so. How about you?"

She sat up, peering around. At first she could not see him. "Cliff! Are you hurt?"

Rubble stirred a few yards away, and Cliff

Hawk's whisper said, "I don't quite know. Something fell on me."

"Oh, Cliff!" Molly struggled to her feet, limped, half crawled across the piles of debris that were all that was left of Hawk's orderly laboratory. "Can you move? Are you in pain?"

A trash heap stirred again, and Molly saw that what she had taken for another heap of litter was the upper part of Hawk's body, powdered with grime and ash, but apparently intact. He seemed to be jackknifed over something, some large object that was resting on what would have been his lap, facing away from her. He twisted and looked at her. It took all his strength, and his face was a mask of effort and pain. "My—legs are caught," he gritted.

"Wait. No, sit still—let me!" And forgetting her own aches she flew to free him; but it was impossible. A beam had fallen across his legs, knocking him down; some other blow had thrust him sidewise. His upper body and arms were filthy and battered, but they were free and he could move. But his legs were under half a ton of mass.

He gave up the effort and slumped forward again, across the weight that pinned him down. After a moment he said, "Where's the Reefer? He can help ..."

Molly looked around helplessly. "I don't know."

"Call him!"

But though she shouted, there was no answer. She stood up, stretching out an arm to the tunnel wall to steady herself. The smoke was getting very thick; something bad was happening in the interior of the workshop, and she could feel a warning of heat.

She shouted for the Reefer again; still no answer.

There was no help for it; if Cliff Hawk was going to get out of the trap that bound him, she was the one who would have to do it. She bent dizzily to tug again at the beam. Hawk did not speak; his eyes were closed, he seemed to be unconscious. The beam was immobile.

Molly knelt in the litter, careless of the jagged edges that were shredding her knees, and methodically began to move what could be moved: the plastic housing from one of Hawk's instrument panels, a tangle of light metal tubing, a drift of shattered glassware. The smoke made her cough and blink, but she did not look up . . .

Not until she became aware of the sound that had been growing in her ears for seconds, loud now, close, compelling. It was a singing rustle like a breeze through dry brush.

The sleeth.

She turned, and froze. The creature hung in the air not a yard from her back, its broad, blind eyes fastened on her, its supple muscles rippling down the black, sleek skin.

For a moment she thought it was help.

But Cliff Hawk did not stir. There was no sign of the Reefer. She was alone with a helpless man, and a creature from space whose whole anatomy was designed for killing.

Under the mountain the flowing essence of power that was the infant rogue star paused to consider the meaning of the sharp-edged triple slap the sun had administered to its curiosity. It was a rebuke, clearly enough. Even at ninety-odd million miles, Sol could have launched a far more devastating blow. The tiny rogue knew that as surely as it knew its own strength, and knew therefore, in its simple logic, that the intent of the blow was not destruction but a warning. *Star too big.* It corrected itself. *I too small. Get bigger.*

It had not been hurt in any way by the triple blast of coiled white flame. It did not fear a harder blow; indeed, it had not evolved a concept of "fear." But there were smaller, more controllable assemblies of particles closer at hand, and the rogue elected to investigate them.

Molly's little car it scanned, solved, manipulated and discarded. (The little vehicle started up at the rogue's remote command, obediently moved forward and, when the rogue withdrew its attention, mindlessly ground ahead until one wheel dropped over the lip of the road and it slid, rolled and finally bounced to destruction down the mountain.)

More complex creations existed, the rogue found. It did not "see," it did not distinguish visible light from any other form of radiation, but it recognized differences in frequency and kind. The differences between the kinds of radiation that were emanated by living creatures were to it something like colors are to carbon-based life: it recognized a "green" glow which flickered violently, as though in fear or pain; a blue-violet aura which waned as the rogue observed it; emanations of all rainbow colors, and far into the infra- and ultra-frequencies, which were the sleeth, a colony of burrowing moles, an ant's nest, even small faintly radiant points, like dust in a searchlight beam, that were the microorganisms in the air, the soil, the bodies of the larger life-forms nearby.

Something about the "green" light interested the

rogue; perhaps it was the violence of its aura. It observed closely, and discovered that there was an organized mass of particulate matter attached to it; the matter seemed to be acting upon that other mass of matter which appeared to be associated with the dwindling blue-violet glow. The rogue observed, without analyzing, certain mechanical vibrations in the surrounding matter that were its sources. *Please, Cliff,* Molly was begging, *help me get you out;* but the rogue was a long way from having formed the concept of communication, much less acquiring a grasp of any language.

A brighter glow of vivid gold was moving toward them; the rogue reached out to encompass it and found it a new phenomenon, something between the car and the humans, far more subtle and complex in its organization than the clumsy mechanical toy it had played with for a moment, then discarded; yet simple enough to be operated. The rogue studied the sleeth for a fraction of a second, then reached out an invisible effector. It played with the sleeth, sending it through the air.

(Outside the cave mouth, the Reefer picked himself up, staggered to his feet and stared wildly about. There was blood on his grimy yellow beard, and his huge features had new scars. He croaked a question at the world, but there was no one to answer, no one in sight, nothing but gray smoke from inside the cave and crackling flame and white smoke from where something had set the cave mouth beams afire. He turned slowly, unsteady on his feet. The sun was a frightening color, roiled red and angry. The sky was clouded and ominous. He shouted for his sleeth, but there was no answer.)

The infant rogue was aware of the dull, slate-colored hue that was the Reefer. It had even recognized a connection between it and its new toy, the sleeth.

It would be interesting, the young rogue thought, to play with one of these more complex mechanisms too.

But for the moment it had not yet tired of the sleeth, arrowing it through the smoky sky, lashing out with its death-dealing claws and transflection fields at birds, rocks, tufts of grass.

The organization of matter fascinated the rogue. It decided to explore the possibilities of changing that organization, of interfering. It decided to be a god.

It thought for a moment of commandeering the Reefer for practice, as it had commandeered and operated first the electrocar, then the sleeth. It considered destroying one of the glowing living things. Any one. Destroying it so that it might be dissected and studied.

But it did not.

Already, only minutes after its first birth from its womb of plasma, the rogue had begun to develop habit patterns and "character." Its development was not only rapid but exponential. Its first actions had been entirely random, as pure a free will as a pinball machine. But it learned. The new and generally unpleasant environment in which it found itself, it had discovered, responded pleasingly to certain kinds of manipulation. It was easy to destroy its features, one by one. The rogue could demolish a rock, kill a living thing, uproot a mountain, lash out at a sun. But once destroyed, it had learned, they were gone.

A more interesting, that is to say a more educational way of manipulating them was to operate short of destruction. To interfere, but not to kill.

Not at first.

There was no question of conscience in this, of course, nor of mercy. The rogue was as yet totally without a superego. But it had learned the sweet taste of pleasure.

These organized masses of matter could be sources of pleasure.

Molly dared move slightly, craning her neck to see past the sleeth.

"Reefer?" she whispered. "Are you there? Can you help me?"

But there was no human figure behind the great singing shadow of the sleeth. It hung there with its huge eyes fastened on her, and then, without warning, slipped forward, darted to the wall, and hung over Cliff Hawk's unconscious body.

Molly screamed, "Don't hurt him!" But in fact the sleeth was not attacking. It bobbed silently over him for a moment, then the pale radiance of its transflection field flickered.

Cliff Hawk's body quivered, then sat slowly up. "Cliff!" cried Molly, "you're all right!" But he was not conscious. His head lolled on a shoulder, his eyes were closed.

She stared wide-eyed at the sleeth. It was lifting Cliff, but why? What was it going to do?

She did not have to wait for an answer. The transflection fields flickered again, and the great beam that had pinned him came up off his lap. It lifted at one end, like the boom of a crane, raised itself to the height of his head, rotated majestically, and dropped into a pile of rubble.

Gently Hawk's torso was allowed to sink back, until he was lying outstretched and unencumbered. He had not regained consciousness.

"Thank you," whispered Molly to the sleeth— knowing it could not understand; not caring whether it could or not. Then she flew to Hawk.

He was badly hurt, but he was alive. There was not much blood. His legs, though, were badly injured; though they lay straight enough, when she moved one he groaned sharply in his sleep and his face twisted in pain.

He needed medical attention. "Oh, Cliff!" she sobbed. "If only you hadn't . . ."

From the cave mouth the voice of the Reefer muttered, "Leave him be. You're as bad hurt as he is."

"Oh, Reefer!" cried the girl. "Help me! Cliff's been badly hurt, and we've got to get him to Wisdom Creek." Then what he had said penetrated to her and she realized, surprised, that she was herself on the verge of unconsciousness. The smoky air made her lightheaded; she was coughing without knowing she was coughing; her bruised, racked body was beginning to hurt in earnest.

"How?" growled the Reefer.

"I don't know!" She swayed dizzily, and wailed, "At least let's get him out in the open. He'll suffocate in here."

The Reefer moved cautiously forward. Even in her misery, Molly could see that he had been hurt himself. His little eyes were sunk in pain; his yellow beard and mustache clotted with blood. He stood over Cliff Hawk, studying him without touching him.

"Can't," he said.

"You've got to!"

"Can't move him. If the sleeth was acting right— but he's not. Spooked fair. Not that I blame him," the Reefer rumbled. "We've chewed up pyropods out in the reefs, but we never tangled with a star before."

"Star? What star?"

"The sun, girl. That triple sunbolt. I think we've got ourselves in trouble."

The sleeth, which had been hanging humming nearby, surged suddenly toward them. The Reefer flinched away, and the sleeth passed him by and darted out into the open air again. "You see, girl? Won't mind me a bit. Don't know what's got into him."

"Then you and I must lift him out!"

The Reefer spat into the rubble. "You? Couldn't lift yourself, I'd say; you're worn out. And I can't manage him by myself. Kill him if I tried."

"Then what can we do? Please, Reefer."

The Reefer looked past her, into the denser smoke that was rolling toward them down the tunnel. "Only one thing I know," he growled. "Shoot him for you, if you like. Better than letting him burn."

The rogue tired of the sleeth, thought for a moment of destroying it, then merely abandoned it to its own devices. It amused itself briefly by examining the state of those nonradiant assemblages of matter which had been so brutally tossed about by the sunbolts. It did not recognize them as instruments, machines, bits of human inventiveness; but it did see that they had been made functionless by the damage they had suffered, and that the chemical reactions now taking place in and among them were damaging them still further.

It understood, after a meditation of some nanoseconds, that the course of the fire was carrying it toward those radiant masses which it had not yet learned to think of as living. It did, however, realize that the same sort of damage that had blasted the machines would harm them as well; and that one of the radiances was visibly fading in any case.

It would be interesting, thought the infant rogue, to do something new. It had already removed the radiationless lump of matter from the radiant mass that was Cliff Hawk, using the sleeth as its proxy; that had been disappointing, nothing had happened.

But, it wondered, what if it were to soak up some of that radiation?

It was a notion that attracted the rogue. It did not know why. It had not yet learned to recognize hunger.

XIV

First the robot required them to wait while it completed its minute of silent adoration, bobbing in its transflection field under the star-embossed dome of the church, its plasma rippling with the colors of devotion. Then it insisted on shepherding each of the children out of the building, locking the doors behind them, searching each empty room and corridor to make sure none had been forgotten. The church was homeostatic, of course; its receptors and proprioceptors could have taken care of all of that without attention. Then the robot proposed another delay while it transmitted an apparently endless message to Deneb; and all the while the boy, Rufe, was chattering with questions and eagerness, and Andy Quam's patience had long gone up in wrath. "Robot Inspector," he shouted, "if we're going, let's go! Molly Zaldivar may be in great danger, even dying!"

The robot swung toward him. "Monitor Quamodian," it sang, "patience! I assure you she is alive."

"How do you know?" he demanded.

The robot was silent.

"Preacher," the boy whispered, "leave him alone. That's the way he is. Does things at his own pace. Say! Are you going to ride his back?"

"Almalik! How do I know?" groaned Andy Quam. He glanced at his wrist timepiece, converted rapidly to Terrestrial equivalents, and hissed with exasperation. "In three hours Starday will be over. I won't need him then! But," he added painfully, tapping his foot on the tiled floor, "Molly needs me *now*."

The robot sang, "Monitor Quamodian, please be silent. I am having a most interesting discussion with three living companions on a planet of Deneb, eight robots and the star 61 Cygni."

"No!" roared Quamodian in astonishment. "You're not chattering away at a time like this! But you promised . . ."

The robot paused. Then, petulantly, "Oh, very well. Perhaps we may as well go, since your noise is disturbing me. Please follow . . ."

But it was too late for following; Andy Quam was already out the door, leaping toward the place where he had left his flyer, and the boy was trailing after him like a comet tail.

"I'll lead the way," sang the robot, raising the amplification of its external vocalizers until the church facade echoed. "I have instructed your guiding apparatus that the hundred-meter limit may be waived, as part of my voluntary Starday activity, permitted under the compact . . ."

Even at ninety decibels Andy Quam didn't hear the end of the sentence; he was already in the flyer, the boy close behind. He slammed the door and shouted, "Let's go! Follow that robot!"

"All right, Mr. Quamodian," cheerfully agreed the voice of his flyer. "I have my clearance now. Say! Wasn't it nice of the robot inspector to let you . . ."

"Shut up," snarled Andy Quam. "Just fly! I'm in a hurry."

Sulkily the flyer lifted itself off the ground, spun round like a top and aimed itself toward the waiting ovoid that was the robot, hanging in its transflection fields a few meters over the Starchurch. Quamodian muttered a curse as he picked himself up from where the sudden gyration had thrown him, the boy in his lap; but he said nothing to the flyer. "You sit there," he ordered Rufe. "Strap yourself in. Almalik knows what this stupid flyer will do next."

Aggrieved, the flyer began, "That's not fair. Mr. Qua . . ."

"I told you to shut up!"

The flyer shut up, with an audible, and intentional click and rasp of static, and Andy Quam and the boy peered away. It was full night, with bright stars hanging over the hills, though to the west the angry red glare of the swollen, surly sun was still faintly visible, bloodying the sky over the horizon. Suddenly the boy grabbed Quamodian's arm.

"There, preacher! See it? That's where the sun-bolts struck."

"I see," Andy Quam ground out. "Flyer, can't we go any faster?"

Resentfully the voice clicked itself on. "No," it said, and clicked off again.

"Now, stop that!" shouted Quamodian. "Why not?"

The flyer relented. "The robot inspector has issued orders for us to follow it," it pointed out. "If I go any faster, it will be following us." Its voice mellowed as it settled down for a nice chat. "You see, Mr. Quamodian," it said, "it is still Starday, and the Robot Inspector does not wish to offend the peace of Starday with a sonic boom. This planet has a rather dense atmosphere, composed principally of oxygen (twenty per cent), nitrogen (eighty per cent), water vapor, carbon dioxide. . ."

"Skip that part! I know Earth's atmosphere!"

"Of course. The point is, Mr. Quamodian, that at these parameters of altitude, temperature and barometric pressure, the sonic barrier occurs at just a bit over our present speed. So you see, no, Mr. Quamodian, we cannot go any faster—and in any event," it added chattily, "we are there."

The flyer deposited them on the side of the mountain; the robot inspector would not allow it any closer to the cave mouth. Andy Quam and the boy piled out, stared upward at the wreck. "Stars, preacher! They really got it!" whispered the boy. "I—I'm afraid Miss Zaldivar was hit."

"We have no such information," sang the robot, humming overhead. "Please wait. I am scanning the area."

But Andy Quam was past the point of caring what the robot inspector wanted. He thrust the boy aside and scrambled up the side of the hill, over uneven ground. He dodged around the wreck of a vehicle—then realized it must be Molly Zaldivar's and stopped, his heart in his mouth, until a frantic search convinced him she was not in it, nor anywhere around. Then up that hill again, his legs pumping, his heart pounding, his breath rasping.

Although in truth, reason was saying in his ear, it was past the time for haste. Whatever destruction had been accomplished here, and it was vast, was long over. Coarse brown smoke oozed from the cave mouth above, and there was a stink of charred plastic and smoldering trash of a thousand kinds. But the fire had burned itself out. No one was in sight.

He paused, his lungs seared with the violence of his breathing, and forced himself to shout, "Molly! Are you here?"

The robot voice sang startlingly from just behind him, "She is fifty meters to your right, Monitor

Quamodian, and just above us. But do not approach."

Andy Quam was already on his way, scrambling around the lip of the little ledge before the cave mouth.

"No wait! There are unpredictable entities about, Monitor Quamodian. A beast from space. And—" the singing whine of the robot faltered, "the rogue star. Allow me to study them!"

Andy Quam snorted, but made no other answer. He slid on loose gravel, caught himself and ran on. It was a forty-foot drop, he had just escaped death, but he had not even noticed it in his haste to find Molly Zaldivar. But where was she?

And then he stopped, sliding and waving his arms to keep from falling.

Something like a giant black squid was leaping toward him, up over the rubble and the smoke, shimmering in a pale transflection field. In the dim starlight he caught a glimpse of great blind eyes staring at him, claws that could rip the guts out of a pyropod. "Monitor Quamodian!" sang the robot peremptorily from behind. "That creature is a sleeth. Do not, I caution you, approach it!"

There was suddenly a sour, coppery taste of fear in Quamodian's mouth. A sleeth—now he recalled the stories about those space beasts, evolved for killing, powerful beyond human competition. If it took a mind to attack him there would be no hope.

But it seemed to have no such intention. It hung there studying him, almost as though it had intelligence, even empathy, even understanding of his haste. Then, as though it were giving permission, it lifted up and away on its transflection fields and hung waiting, a hundred meters up, no longer between him and the little hummock where he could see shadowy forms.

He spared the sleeth no more thought, but scrambled, slid and trotted the remaining distance and dropped to his knees beside the girl who had summoned him across half the known universe. "Molly!" he cried. "What's happened? What have they done to you?"

He crooked an arm under her head, raised her tenderly.

And her eyes opened.

She looked at him wonderingly, like a child awakened from sleep. Her face was bloody, scratched, smudged with soot and filth. Her hair was flying loose as chaff on a breeze, and her clothes were shredded into rags. But suddenly and gloriously she smiled at him. "Why, it's little Andy Quam," she whispered. "I should have known you'd come."

The smile lingered, briefly only. Then, without warning, her face twisted, the smile fled, she turned her head away. And Molly Zaldivar wept as though her heart would break.

"Robot Inspector!" shouted Andy Quam. "Where is that fool machine?"

From the side of a boulder, ten feet away, a small voice said querulously, "He's gone, preacher. Just zipped away. Almalik knows where. Didn't say a word."

"What are you doing here, Rufe?" Andy Quam demanded. "You should stay in the flyer. Well, as long as you're here, give me a hand. Miss Zaldivar's been hurt. We've got to get her to help . . ."

A figure disengaged itself from the gloom and stepped closer. "No hurry about that, friend," it rumbled. "She lived through this much, she'll live a while yet."

Quamodian jumped to his feet, ready for anything. He peered into the darkness, caught a glimpse of dulled yellow mustache, dingy yellow beard, a face that looked as though planets had rolled over it in their orbits. "Who the devil are you?" he barked.

"Talk big for a little fellow, don't you?" rasped the voice. "No harm. No hard feelings." He stepped closer and Quamodian got the measure of the size of him, a giant of a man, but oddly subdued. "No one around here wants trouble," he added in a mild bass growl. "Not any more. But the girl's all right, I got her out of the tunnel before she got hurt."

Quam said suspiciously, "I heard something about a Reefer up here with Cliff Hawk, doing Almalik knows what foul work. Are you him?"

"I am."

"Then that's your sleeth watching us up there."

The Reefer's mustache and beard parted company. In the gloom it looked almost as though he were preparing to bite Andy Quam, but it was only a soundless, humorless laugh. "Not mine any more," he declared. "His own by now, I expect. Or—something's. But he won't take orders from me, not since the sun hit us." He turned aside from Andy Quam, bent for a moment over the girl. "She's all right," he said, straightening, but his voice didn't sound very sure. "You might be right about getting her out of here, though. Me too, if you don't mind."

"Why is Molly Zaldivar crying like that?" Quamodian demanded. "If you've hurt her . . ."

The great head shook from side to side. "Nothing I did," he said. "I expect it's Cliff Hawk she's crying about."

Quamodian pulled himself together; he had completely forgotten that Hawk was here! It was his fault, no doubt, that Molly Zaldivar had been hurt, endangered, terrified; yet there was still enough friendship left between Quamodian and Cliff Hawk for Andy Quam's voice to show real concern as he asked, "What about Hawk? Is he hurt?"

"Not any more."

"What? You mean—dead?"

The great voice tolled leadenly. "Not that either. Worse, I'd say. A *lot* worse. And if you want my opinion, we ought to get away from here before something worse happens to us, too."

The Something that had been a random mass of stripped electrons, then an infant rogue star, then a seeking, learning, experimenting entity—and was now something else—"watched" the Reefer and Andy Quam gently lift the weeping girl, carry her down the slope to the flyer, hastily enter, slam the door and race away.

With one part of itself, the rogue caused the sleeth to soar after them on its transflection fields, keeping the flyer effortlessly in view. It was not necessary to do that, of course. The rogue could easily have kept the flyer under observation with its probes, anywhere on the face of this planet and indeed almost anywhere in this solar system. (It had not yet had occasion to try to perceive anything farther away than the planets.)

But it was no longer the simple creature it had been.

When it had perceived that one of the organized radiant masses was in danger of extinction it had occurred to its still simple mind that it might be worth acquiring, and so it had acquired it. It turned out to be easy—a "stretch," a "grasp," a "hold." If it had been matter doing these things, one might have said that it was like the flow of an amoeba, en-globing and digesting a tasty bit of food. Matter was not involved, and the forces that the rogue deployed did not lend themselves to description in three-space geometry.

But the effect was the same.

What had once been the persona of Cliff Hawk no longer inhabited its biological body. That body, in fact, was not merely dead but by now an unrecogniz-able lump of contorted charcoal, mixed with the other charred and destroyed litter in the burned-out tunnel that had once been Hawk's workshop.

But something of him remained. It no longer had identity of its own, as an individual. But it was at least a perceptible fraction of that seething, restless entity that surged through the interstices of the mountain, that followed Andy Quam's flyer in the person of the sleeth, that had brought the wrath of the sun striking down on the summit of the hill, that was a newborn rogue star loosed in the universe.

It no longer "thought" in simple urges and obser-vations.

Through the trained intelligence of its human component it now could observe, analyze, record— and act.

It sensed the wonder of that far-off watcher.

XV

Technically it was still Starday; at the boy's suggestion Andy Quam ordered the flyer to take them to the Starchurch. "There'll be a crowd for late-night services," he said, "and likely enough nobody's going to be where you expect them, otherwise. I mean, even the hospital might not have a crew on duty."

"Shocking," hissed Andy Quam. "To make the Companionship of the Star a pagan ritual!"

"Sure, preacher. Like you say. Only that's the way it is, so you better . . ."

"I understand," said Quam, and gave the flyer its directions. It raised an objection.

"Without the special permission of the robot inspector, Mr. Quamodian," it declared, "I should properly go nowhere except back to the transflex terminal."

"But it's an emergency!"

"Of course, Mr. Quamodian." It hesitated, its neural currents pondering the problem. "Since I cannot contact the robot inspector at the moment," it decided. "I will have to return to the transflex terminal . . ."

"Confound you," shouted Quamodian, "Do what I tell you!"

". . . but en route I will pause briefly at the

101

Starchurch. If you then disembark, it is not a matter under my control."

"Hah!" barked Quamodian in disgust. "Do it, then. But do it fast!"

"It is done, Mr. Quamodian," sighed the flyer, settling to the ground. "I will remain here for one minute. During that time you may do as you wish."

Quamodian wasted no more time in talk. With Rufe and the huge, slow strength of the Reefer, it was no problem to get Molly out of the flyer and settle her gently on the ground. "Are you all right, dear?" Andy Quam asked anxiously. "I'm going for help . . ."

The storm of weeping had passed. Her eyes were open and her face composed, but the weariness of ages was in her eyes. "All right, Andy," she said. "I'm all right anyway, so it doesn't matter."

"Don't talk like that!"

"All right, Andy," she repeated dully, and looked away.

"You stay here with her," he ordered the Reefer, who looked resentfull but shrugged. "Rufe, let's find somebody!" And the man and the boy hurried into the Starchurch.

As they entered the great chamber under the blue dome, a gong boomed and echoed. Rufe led the way, up a helical ramp into the dim vast church. The air was alive with the throb of many chanting voices, and sweet with the odor of the fusorian Visitants. The five pointed wings of the place of worship were filled with rising tiers of seats, but every seat was empty. The people were kneeling in concentric circles on the immense floor, beneath the central dome that held the imaged suns of Almalik.

Of the robot inspector there was no sign. His errand, whatever it was, still kept him away.

"I see Molly's aunt!" cried Rufe eagerly, pointing. "Come this way!"

But Quamodian hesitated. "Pagan ritual" he called it, but something in the air held him, awed, faintly envious, half afraid. He raised his eyes to the many-colored splendor of the thirteen suns hung beneath the space-black inside of the dome: six close binaries arranged in three double doubles, one single sun.

Drinking in the blazing beauty of Almalik, breathing the sweetness of the Visitants, swaying to the melodic rhythm of the chanting worshippers, Andy Quam felt a sudden glorious dawn of utter peace and great joy. He wanted to forget himself and the waiting, weary girl outside. His only desire was to forget himself and to be one with Almalik.

"Preacher!" hissed the boy. "Aren't you coming?"

Solemn awe held Quamodian. "Are—are you sure it's all right to interrupt?"

"We won't interrupt. I've been here before for this, to watch, like. With Miss Zaldivar. They don't mind anybody."

Shivering with the strange elation, Quamodian followed the boy out across the vast floor and into the circles of communicants swaying on their knees. The sweetness of the Visitants made him drowsy; the blazing suns of Almalik bathed him in peace.

But the boy had paused before a kneeling man and woman. "Here's her folks, preacher," he said. "Mr. Juan Zaldivar. Mrs. Deirdre Zaldivar." His thin voice rose sharply. "This is Monitor Quamodian."

103

They stopped their chant. Reluctantly they withdrew their gaze from the multiple splendor of Almalik and, still swaying on their knees, looked incuriously at Andy Quam.

Both glowed with youth and health and joy. Juan was lean and tall and dark, with rich black hair. Blonde, blue-eyed and radiant, Deirdre looked even younger and more lovely than her daughter.

And both wore the mark of Almalik, where the migrating fusorian colony had entered their bodies. Deirdre's was on her blooming cheek, Juan's on his forehead. The marks were tiny irregular star shapes, their edges dissolving into fine branching lines. In the dusk of the starlit dome, the marks glowed softly, warmly golden.

"It's about Molly," Quamodian whispered, hardly daring to break the spell. "She's outside. She's hurt." Incongruous things to say in this sacred peace! He felt more of an interloper than ever, a brute among angels.

In unison, blonde and black, they nodded their heads. Puzzled, Andy Quam started to repeat what he had said, but Deirdre breathed, "There's no hurt that matters in the bosom of the Star. She must join us, and then she will find peace."

"But she's hurt! It's—oh, it's too long to tell you, but she's in terrible danger. We all are!"

"Not here," smiled Juan Zaldivar. He groped for Deirdre's hand; she was already lifting her face to chant again. "Bring her within. The Visitants will make her whole!" And his dark eyes lifted and he joined his wife in the chant.

Rufe bit his lip. "It's no use, preacher," he said somberly. "They're too happy."

Andy Quam looked at him meditatively. It was, after all, not a bad idea to bring Molly inside, he thought. Let the Visitants enter her body with their fusorian healing. She would heal; everyone did. Not merely the scuffs and bruises of her body, but the somber agony of her mind . . .

"Preacher," whispered the boy apprehensively, staring at him.

Quamodian caught himself. "Sorry," he mumbled, and grabbed the boy's elbow, turned him around, scurried away. He felt a sudden flood of longing that almost stopped him and turned him back, but the boy was leading him now. He stumbled out of the aura of Almalik, down the helical ramp, out of the building as the siren chant faded behind.

Quamodian filled his lungs gratefully with cool dry air that held no lotus odor of the Visitants.

He said sadly, "I wanted to stay. I always want to stay. But it isn't for me—the peace of Almalik." He hurried down the ramp, leaving a vanishing vague regret.

His flyer was gone, but the huge form of the Reefer stood solidly over the reclining body of Molly Zaldivar. The night air felt suddenly chill, and Andy Quam shivered. "What can we do now?" he muttered, half to himself. "What can we do for Molly Zaldivar?"

"My house, preacher," said the boy, Rufe. "It's only down the square, over there. My folks will take her in. I think," he added, sounding worried. Andy Quam glanced at him sharply, but did not question him.

However, there was no one at home in the house to which the boy led them. The door was unlatched.

Lights were on. The little cottage's autonomic living systems were purring away, a cheery fire in the hearth, a pleasantly scented breath of air carrying the gentle warmth to every room. But no one was there. "Never mind," sighed the boy, as though he had expected it. "I expect what Miss Zaldivar mostly needs is a little rest right now. Why don't you take her in that room, preacher? And I'll see if I can stir up a little food; you must be hungry."

Fed, warmed, almost relaxed, Andy Quam sat in the cheerful living room. The boy lay on the floor before the fire, his chin in his hands, stretching out now and then for another piece of fruit or a last crumb of the sandwiches he had produced for them. And the Reefer leaned at his ease against the fireplace, answering Quamodian's questions.

They had begun like a prosecuting attorney and defendant; but the Reefer would not accept the role. Defiant, uncaring, mildly contemptuous of everything around him, the Reefer rumbled, "I'll not take the responsibility, Monitor Quamodian. What happens on my land is my business, and those hills are mine."

"Creating rogue life is everyone's business," cried Quamodian.

"But that was not my doing," the big man declared. His scarred face was angry. "Miss Zaldivar is a lovely child. I meant no harm for her. But she had no business trespassing."

"What about Cliff Hawk?"

Under the ragged beard, his mouth set hard. "I brought his mother back from the reefs. He was almost a son to me—but I take no blame for what he has done. Except that I let him go to school, but that wasn't my intention. I wanted him to be another hunter, like me. When he was grown, I planned to take him back to the reefs, find a cub sleeth for him, let him do as I did. But he had to cross the creek. He went to Starday school. He got queer ideas from the robots and the Visitants. Finally he had to go away to space to learn to be what you call a tran-science engineer . . ."

"There was nothing wrong with that," declared Quamodian. "I was at the same school. He was a decent human being then."

The Reefer shrugged; then, flinching, touched his arm where it was bandaged. "No matter," he rumbled moodily. "He's paid for it now. He's dead. Or so I think."

"What do you mean, you *think?*" demanded Quamodian. "Is he dead or isn't he?"

The Reefer's deep-set eyes peered at him from under the bushy yellow brows. "He wasn't breathing," he said shortly. "Does that answer your question?"

"Doesn't it?"

The Reefer said helplessly, "I don't know, Monitor, and that's the truth. Oh, Cliff was in bad shape, all right. I didn't give him much chance of lasting more than an hour—less, because we couldn't move him and the fire was coming close. But . . ."

He hesitated. "Boy," he growled, "have you got anything to drink in this place?"

"Just milk. Or water. Or maybe I could make a cup of tea . . ."

The Reefer pursed his lips, shook his head gloomily.

"Go on!" ordered Quamodian.

The Reefer half closed his eyes. "Cliff had been at work in his transcience lab," he droned, apparently bored with the subject. "I knew what he was doing was dangerous, but he's a man grown now. Was. I didn't want to interfere. Then something happened."

The Reefer shifted position, thoughtfully scratched his bushy yellow head. The thick fingers raked through the blond tangles like gangplows through soil, methodically, deeply, mechanically. He said, "It was an explosion. Down below, in the old cryomagnetic and radiation galleries that used to be part of the Plan of Man's military installations. Things the Visitants had failed to destroy. That was the part that I knew was dangerous. Then, while we were putting ourselves together, Molly Zaldivar showed up, crying and threatening Cliff; she'd been scared by my sleeth, so I guess she wasn't accountable. But that was just the beginning. There was a real blowup then. Don't know where. Something winged me—a stray piece of metal, I guess, and I was knocked out for a while."

"I was watching from Wisdom Creek," said Quamodian. "I saw a bolt of plasma strike from the sun, then two more. Is that what it was?"

"I guess." The Reefer scratched again stolidly. "Then I heard Cliff and the girl inside. I went to them. Tried to call my sleeth, but the creature was spooked, acted funny, didn't respond. It never did that before. But there it was, inside the tunnel, trying to get Cliff uncovered. Only it was too late. He was dying. Then . . ."

The Reefer stood up straighter and stopped scratching. A look of real humanity came into his eyes as he said bleakly, "Cliff looked up at me. He said something—couldn't hear what, exactly. It didn't make sense. And he just stopped breathing."

The Reefer turned away, began roaming around the little room. "I don't mean he just died then, Monitor. I've seen men die; they make a little more fuss about it than that. But he just *stopped*. Like he was turned off. And I made sure he was dead, and then I grabbed Molly Zaldivar and got out of there. 'Bout an hour later, you showed up. That's it."

"Not quite," said Andy Quam sharply. "What was it that Cliff said before he died?"

The Reefer stopped, stared angrily at him. "Doesn't matter! It didn't make sense, anyway."

"What was it?"

The Reefer growled wordlessly. The thick fingers plowed into the scalp again, raked it furiously. Then he dropped his hand and said, "Oh, if you must know—it was something like, 'I made it—now it wants me.' "

Quam abruptly shivered, as though a cold blast had found the back of his neck. "What does it mean?" he demanded.

"Nothing! Nothing at all, Monitor! Or anyway—" the Reefer looked away, "nothing that I understand. 'I made it—now it wants me.' Does it mean anything to you?"

Quamodian paused before answering. "I—hope not," he whispered.

The rogue was no longer an infant. Neither was it full grown—call it a youth, becoming steadily larger, each moment finding itself stronger and more skilled than the moment before, feeding upon everything around it that offered energy or mass or patterns to be assimilated.

It had now assimilated a very large number of patterns, sipping at the assorted radiances that surrounded it, and in the process discovering that some were far—"tastier"?—than others. Engorging the identity that had once been Cliff Hawk had been a transcendentally new experience for it, and now it found itself equipped with a thousand new habit patterns, constructs of thought, programmatic drives. They no longer had any relationship to the hundred kilograms of carbon compounds that had been Cliff Hawk's physical body, for that was now an irrelevant blob of spoiled reactions. Hawk's "personality," even, was gone—nothing now remained in the universe that thought his thoughts, remembered his experiences, could recite his opinions. But something of his motives and desires remained as a moment of thrust inside the behavior of the young rogue, shaping the vector result that was its behavior. It was no longer entirely random. In some degree it had become polarized.

What were the other moments of force that played a part in the behavior of the infant rogue? Its own growing knowledge and skills. Its discoveries about the world it lived in. Its innate drive toward growth and mastery. *Move. Grow. Eat,* it had thought, as soon as it could think at all; but now, with the powerful discipline of Cliff Hawk's trained mind permeating its being, it thought more clearly and articulately; it had discovered the convenience of formulating its objectives in language.

I am small but I am growing, thought the maturing rogue star that had been born on earth. *There*

*are other beings which are large but do not grow. I
can be more powerful than they.*

And already it had implemented its strength with
a dozen organized masses of matter. The sleeth was
now its mind-linked tool; it watched with the rogue's
eyes, would act under the rogue's wishes. Tiny
crawling and flying things, in the mountain, under
the mountain and in the air above it, had all become
a part of its extended being. And it had recruited
something else.

For the robot inspector had challenged the curiosity of the rogue. It had not been difficult at all for
the rogue to swallow it whole, to incorporate the
mind analogue of the machine into its own consciousness. The robot still looked as it had, torpedo-
shaped metal body and glowing plasma panel; but it
was no longer its links with the supercomputers on
the planets of the stars of Almalik that gave it its
categorical imperatives, but the needs and intentions
of the stripped electron plasma that had exploded
under the hill.

The rogue toyed with and puzzled over, but did
not yet understand that complex linkage of transflection fields which united this new part of its
self with distant and more powerful beings. They did
not matter at the moment. The distant entities were
not powerful enough to resume control against the
near and mighty presence of the rogue. And it had
other considerations to occupy it.

One was a part of its heritage from the dying mind
of Cliff Hawk. Over that too the rogue puzzled,
without comprehension.

Why was it that it felt so attracted, so drawn to, so
conscious of the presence of that small and unimpor-

tant organized mass of thought-radiant matter that Cliff Hawk's mind had indentified as "Molly Zaldivar"?

Through the blind, transflex eyes of the sleeth riding high over the cottage where Molly Zaldivar lay sleeping, the mind of the rogue stared down. *Molly Zaldivar,* it thought, *what do I want with you?*

And inside the house Molly started up from sleep and tried to scream. *Sleep,* ordered the rogue; and the girl subsided into the catalepsy of terror. No one had heard her scream; no one was in the house at that moment, and she had not been able to be loud enough to reach those who were outside on the grass, staring up at the sleeth.

The boy said, awed, "Mister, that's a wicked-looking beast. You sure it won't hurt us?"

The Reefer barked a savage laugh. "Not any more, boy," he rumbled. "Time was that sleeth would follow me like a kitten. Do everything I wanted it to, never think of disobeying—I raised it from a cub, it never knew any boss but me. But now it does." He studied the sleeth thoughtfully for a moment. As it hung in the sky on its shimmering transflection fields, the great black creature looked like some wingless Pegasus astride the air, its dangling claws capable of wrenching any carbon-based, air-breathing, muscle-powered animal in two as readily as a hawk's talons rend fur. "Fine beast," he said. "But not mine any more."

Andy Quam said angrily, "Why did you bring it here? This sort of animal doesn't belong on a planet!"

112

"Why, because it's mine, Monitor Quamodian," and Reefer said simply. "I'm a hunter, and it's my companion. It goes wherever I go. Or used to. Why," he cried, suddenly enthusiastic, "with that sleeth I collected the finest specimens of every game animal in the solar system! You should have seen them. A score of fine pyropods. Darkbeasts from out past the reefs, moonbats, creatures from the hot deeps of Venus—there was nothing in a dozen light-years could touch that sleeth as a killer!"

Andy Quam said in disgust, "You talk as though killing were a good thing. Violence is evil. The laws of Almalik do not permit the destruction of life by life!"

The Reefer's deep eyes twinkled. "And would you never take a life, Monitor Quamodian? Not even, say, to save Miss Zaldivar?"

Andy Quam flushed. "We Companions are exempt from certain of Almalik's laws," he said stiffly. "We may even admit violence, in some situations."

"Then help me!" cried the Reefer. "I'm going to stalk something new, Monitor Quamodian, and you can join me in the hunt. I don't know what it is that's controlling my sleeth, but I'm going to take its pelt to put in my collection!"

"Nonsense," cried Andy Quam, startled. "Why—great Almalik, man—I mean, how can you? Don't you realize that that's probably a rogue star?"

The Reefer's laughter boomed. "Scare you, Monitor Quamodian?"

"No! Or—yes, maybe. I don't think it is unreasonable of a mere human being to question his ability to deal with a star!"

The boy, who had been watching them silently,

turning from face to face, coughed and interrupted. Changing the subject he said, "Say, preacher! What's the matter with the moon?"

A dozen degrees over the horizon the gibbous moon floated, almost invisible, so dark a red was it. It was leprously stained and discolored, by no means the brilliant white fat crescent it should have appeared.

"It's the sun," said Andy Quam gloomily. "Remember how red and angry-looking it was when it set? After those sunbolts struck? The moon's just reflecting it. And this man thinks he can destroy the thing that did that!"

"Worth a try, Monitor," boomed the Reefer cheerfully. "Mind if I borrow your flyer?"

"For what?"

"Why, for the hunt. It's a bit of a walk from here to the hills on foot," the Reefer apologized. "As I don't have the sleeth to take me there any more, I'd appreciate the use of your flyer. It's long past Starday now, no reason not to use it."

Rufe cried out sharply. "Preacher! Listen—what's that sound?"

Quamodian raised his hand imperiously, silencing the Reefer's booming voice. They listened. Then Quam's face twisted. "It's Molly," he cried, turning to run toward the house. "She's calling my name!"

But when Andy Quam burst through the door of the girl's room she was lying wide-awake, looking at the ceiling. Slowly she lowered her eyes to look at him. "Andy," she said. "I should have known you'd come. I've always been able to rely on you."

Quamodian's ears burned. "Are you all right?" he demanded. "I heard you calling . . ."

She sat up on the edge of the bed. "All right? I suppose so." Her face was a mask of tragedy for a moment. "Poor Cliff," she whispered. "It's strange! I thought he was talking to me, in my dream. But it wasn't really him—it was something huge and strange. A monster." She shook herself.

Then, gloriously, she smiled. There was tragedy beneath the smile, but it was clear to Andy Quam that she was making an effort to be cheerful. "I dragged you all the way across space," she said. "I'm sorry. I've always been a trouble to you, Andy dear."

"Never a trouble," he said, speaking from a depth of passion that shook him. Molly was touched. She reached out and patted his arm. "Is there anything to eat?" she asked, incongruously. "It's been a long time!"

Rufe was happy to oblige when Quamodian relayed the girl's request to him, producing more sandwiches and milk, a seemingly inexhaustible supply of food. "Won't your family mind your taking us in like this?" asked Andy Quam. "We're eating you out of house and home!"

The boy's face clouded. "It's all right, preacher," he said.

Quamodian frowned at him. "Come to think of it," he said, "where are your family? It's pretty late for them to be at the Starchurch."

"Oh, they're not there any more. They—they've gone away for a while."

Andy Quam stopped in the middle of the humming little kitchen, busy generating new supplies of bread and milk and meats to replace those the boy had drawn from its programs, and said firmly, "You're hiding something, Rufe, Why?"

"Aw, don't ask me, preacher. It's just—well, it's kind of private."

But then Molly Zaldivar came out of her room, looking remarkably refreshed and restored, and Andy Quam let the matter drop.

For half an hour they were all at ease, Molly as friendly and affectionate as ever in the old days on Exion Four, the boy beside himself with pleasure at pleasing Molly, even the Reefer almost jolly. The huge man from space demanded to know whether Quamodian would join him in his hunt for the rogue. For a moment, in that warm room, it almost seemed like a reasonable idea, and Quamodian let himself think about it—a long chase, a view-hallo, the quarry at bay. But it was fantasy. This was no beast of the forest but an inimical creature of linked plasmas whose size and might were utterly incomprehensible to humans. To hunt it was like setting a snare for a supernova.

Then Andy Quam saw Molly hiding a yawn, and realized with a start how utterly exhausted he was. "Let's get some sleep," he ordered, and fussed over them all until they had sorted themselves out into various rooms. Only then did Quamodian let himself sprawl out on the couch in the living room, the door to Molly's room just past his head, ready to spring up at any alarm.

It had been a good many hours, and a good many millions of parsecs, since he had slept. When he closed his eyes he was unconscious almost at once, and slept like the dead.

XVI

Where was the rogue? As well try to fix the position of an electron in its blurred orbit around a nucleus; it was under the hill and in it, suffusing the skies around, inhabiting the body of the sleeth that soared tirelessly and patiently over the house where Molly Zaldivar slept, penetrating and entering every hidden place within hundreds of miles, and reaching out into near space.

But if its position had no exact geographic boundaries, at least there were loci of special consequence. It did, for example, occupy the great animal bulk of the sleeth. It concentrated at least a sizable part of its being in the electron cloud that seeped through the rock and clay of the base of the hill. And it found other special areas of interest to toy with.

It found, for one, the antique handling machine that Cliff Hawk had used to help him construct his tunnel workshop. It was a minor puzzle to the rogue, but a faintly interesting one; the machine had obvious purpose, and it spent some moments working out that purpose and how to achieve it. Then, the machine solved, it spent a few moments now in what can only be called pleasure. *Power in motors*, it thought. *My power. Spin gears. Drive through rubble*. It reached out with its metal arms and picked up bits of debris—a yellow cylinder of helium, the half of a thousand-pound armature, bent out of shape in the explosions. It threw them about recklessly, madly . . .

Then it had had all it could enjoy of that particular game, and turned to another.

The robot inspector was a greater puzzle, but a lesser plaything. It was no particular joy to operate, since its transflection drives were too similar to the sleeth's, or the rogue's own, to be novel. But the rogue was aware that somehow the robot had been guided by other influences, far away, and that some part of it was still trying to respond to those influences as their messages crackled into its receptors. They were an irritation to the rogue, these repetitious exhortations on behalf of the star Almalik; it did not like them

It had, by now, begun to acquire emotion.

One particular emotion troubled it, that inexplicable urging toward Molly Zaldivar which it had felt, ever more strongly, as Cliff Hawk's patterns of thought asserted themselves and fitted themselves into the organization of the rogue's own habit-structure. The rogue did not find this incongruous. It had no standards by which to judge incongruity. But it found it troubling.

There was a solution to things which were troubling. It could act on the impulse, and see what came of it.

It could attempt to add Molly Zaldivar to itself.

XVII

"Mol-ly. Mol-ly Zaaal-di-var . . ."

Molly woke slowly, surfacing inch by inch from sleep. She was unwilling to wake up. Sleeping though she was, a part of her mind remembered what waking would bring back to her in utter, unwanted clarity. Cliff's death, the birth of the rogue, the terrible danger that the man she loved had unloosed on the universe.

"Mol-ly . . ."

But someone was calling her name. Resentfully she opened her eyes and looked around.

No one was in the room. It was still dark; she had not slept for more than an hour or two.

"Who is it?" she whispered. No response. Molly shivered. It was eerie, that disembodied voice, unlike any she had ever heard. It was impossible to dismiss it as the ragged end of a dream, half remembered on waking; it was real enough. It was even more impossible to ignore it and go back to sleep.

Molly stood up, threw the robe Rufe had found for her over her shoulders, and padded to the door of her room. She opened it just a crack. There was the living room, with Andy Quam asleep on the couch. He stirred painfully as she looked at him, grimaced, mumbled some sleep-evoked phrase and was still again—all without opening his eyes. Poor

Andy, she thought warmly, and sadly; and closed the door without sound.

Whoever had called her, it was not Andy Quam.

She went to the window, threw back the curtains—and gasped in terror.

There it was, hovering just outside the double French panes on its shimmering transflection fields.

The sleeth!

The great blind eyes stared emptily at her, the metal-tipped claws caught reflections of cold fire from the sinking moon. The shimmering field pulsed rapidly, and from the pane of glass she caught the faint vibration of sound that had called her from sleep: "Mol-ly. Come. I—want—you."

For an instant stark terror flooded her, and she half turned to run, to shake Andy Quam awake and beg for protection against this fantastic monster that called her name. But the utter wondrousness of it held her. The sleeth could not speak; nothing the Reefer had said about it gave it a voice. Nor could it have known her name, not in any way that she could hope to understand. And anyway, the sleeth was no longer even an animal in its own independent right; it was only a captive of the thing that Cliff Hawk had made, and had been killed by.

She flung open one side of the French window. She didn't know why; obviously, if the creature intended her harm, the flimsy glass and frame could not protect her. "What—what do you want?" she breathed.

But it only repeated, "Mol-ly. Mol-ly, come."

The sound came from the glass itself, she discovered; somehow the creature was vibrating to form frequencies that she could hear as words. It was even stranger, she thought, than if it had suddenly formed lips, palate and tongue and spoken to her.

It was terrifying. Worse than terrifying; without warning, she was filled with a revulsion so fierce that she almost screamed with the pain of it.

"No," she whispered. "No!" and closed the window.

"Come," sang the sleeth—or whatever it was that controlled the sleeth. The huge creature danced patiently on its shimmering fields, waiting for her to accede to its demand. "Come," said the tinny, bodiless voice again. "Mol-ly. Come."

Insane to be talking to this thing, in a perfectly ordinary room, through a perfectly normal window! "No!" she said strongly. "Go away!"

Did the thing understand her words? She had no way of knowing. It merely hung there silently for a moment, regarding her with those great blind eyes.

Then it moved, slowly and remorselessly, like a Juggernaut. It bobbed silently forward, thrusting the unopened window out of the way as though it were air. An almost soundless crack and a faint patter of shattered glass on the carpet were the only noise it made as it came toward her.

The great, deadly claws reached for her.

Molly drew a breath to scream, tried to turn and run . . .

Something bright and murderous flashed from those blind eyes. It was like an instant anesthetic, like a blow from behind that drives out awareness before the mind quite realizes it has been struck. Down went Molly Zaldivar into paralysis and dark, stunned and helpless. She felt herself falling, falling, falling . . .

The last thing she remembered was those great claws grasping her. Incredible, she thought, they don't hurt . . .

And then the world closed in around her.

Quamodian woke painfully in broad daylight that poured through the windows. He found himself on a couch, with a synthetic copy of some animal fur over him for warmth, his head throbbing, his bones aching. He felt vaguely ill, and for a moment could not recall where he was.

Then he remembered. The enigma of the sunbolts. The nightmare of the Reefer and the sleeth. The death of Cliff Hawk. The birth of the rogue . . .

He forced himself to sit up and look at the world around him.

Pinned to the arm of the couch was a note, scrawled with a photoscriber in a huge, clumsy hand:

> Preacher, I didn't want to wake you. I went to tell Miss Zaldivar's folks she's all right. Meet you there if you want. P.S., I left everybody sleeping because I thought you all needed it. Food in the kitchen.
>
> Rufe

Sleeping they still were, to judge from the mighty rasping snores that came from the little cubicle Rufe had given the Reefer. There was no sound at all from Molly's room. Andy Quam hesitated, his hand on the door; but there was no sense disturbing her, and surely nothing could have got past him to harm her in the night . . .

He left the house and stepped out into the bright morning.

Bright it was. Yet, thought Andy Quam, there was something strange about it, and in a moment he realized what it was. The colors were wrong. There was no cloud in the sky, but the air had a lowering quality, as of storm clouds. He squinted up at the sun and perceived the reason.

Red, sullen, blotched, the disk of the sun still had not recovered from whatever had roiled it yesterday. It was not the familiar sun of Earth, as men had portrayed it in a thousand books and songs. It was somehow like the snake-haired sun of that far world where he had left Clothilde Kwai Kwich.

He limped across a wide· square, reviving somewhat as he moved. It had been a strenuous day. And a worrisome one, he thought, remembering with wrinkled brow all the unanswered problems and unmet challenges it had offered.

Perhaps this new day would clear some of them up, he thought—but without much confidence.

He gave the Starchurch a wide berth, hailed a passing citizen and found himself directed to the home of Molly Zaldivar's parents. It was past the Central Municipal Plexus, he discovered, which fit in well enough with his plans; he could use more information if he could get it.

But the Central Municipal Plexus did not turn out to be the combination library-town hall he had expected.

He walked across a queerly perfect circle of stained and blackened cement. It was puzzling, it seemed to have no place in this countrified idyll of a town. Immediately a recorded voice spoke to him:

"Welcome, guest! You have landed at Wisdom Creek Historical Monument. It is a section of the original village of Wisdom Creek, reconstructed exactly as it was on the winter day, many years ago, when the Visitants first arrived."

Andy Quam spoke up, addressing his remarks to thin air, for there was no speaker in sight. "I don't want a historical tour," he snapped. "I want some information."

But there was no response. This was a low-grade programmed instructor, he realized with irritation. Not even homeostatic, merely programmed to respond to his mass-sensed presence with a recorded lecture. He walked through a thick gate . . .

And found himself in something that, for a startled moment, made him think he was in Hell. The air stung his eyes. It choked him, with a reek of industrial fumes and imperfectly oxidized mineral fuels. Blinking and squinting, he made out that he was surrounded by grimy rows of hideous little brick and wooden huts.

Far down a street was a human figure, faced away from him and motionless. Vexed, Andy Quam stamped toward it, ignoring the revolting spectacle around him.

He approached a squat gray pile of concrete on which was etched the legend, *Plan of Man*. A voice from the air cried brightly: "Welcome guest! This structure, a part of the Central Municipal Plexus Exhibit, represents a primitive Tax Office. Here each citizen reported to the Plan of Man the number of tokens he had received for his work in the previous sidereal year, whereupon he was forced to give up a share of them. Here too was the ration office, where he received permission to barter what tokens he had left for articles of clothing and other necessities. Here too was the draft office, where young men and women were impressed for training in the use of crude but adequate weapons of the time. Here too was that most central and fundamental institution, the Planning Office, where every action of every citizen was dictated and reviewed and corrected by a primitive central computer. Here, guest, was the very nerve center of the fundamental coercive apparatus of the state!"

Andy Quam trudged grimly on, ignoring the senseless prattle. There was entirely too much realism in this exhibit for his comfort, he thought with distaste. The very air was polluted with the hydrocarbons and fly-ash and photochemicals of primitive combustion products. And the man he was approaching was oddly dressed in what must have been the costume of the time: a thick fiber uniform, a brutally chopped haircut, something about his neck which looked like a massive metal collar, certainly too heavy and too tight to be comfortable. He stood stark still facing the entrance of the building, his right arm raised in a motionless salute.

"Excuse me," called Andy Quam. "Can you help me find the home of Juan Zaldivar?"

He caught himself, realizing at once that it was only a lifelike dummy. Another recording explained cheerfully:

"The human form you see, guest, is the replica of a Risk. So self-directed men and women were designated. The iron collar worn by each Risk contained an explosive decapitation charge, which could be detonated instantly by the Planning Machine in the event of any suspect action."

Soberly, stiffly, the figure dropped its salute, turned until its mass-sensors located Andy Quam and haltingly bowed. "Oh, great Almalik!" cried Quamodian, exasperated. "All I want is directions! How can I reach the home of Mr. and Mrs. Zaldivar?"

Silence, except for the questioning hum of a carrier signal.

"Isn't *anybody* listening?" he shouted.

Silence again, then, doubtfully, "Guest, you are invited to return to the Wisdom Creek Historical Monument, which has been restored and maintained by the Companions of the Star for public information."

"I *am* a Companion of the Star! I am Monitor Andreas Quamodian, and I insist on your answering my question!"

Silence once more. "We hope you found the exhibits instructive," sighed the recorded voice at last. Its programming clearly was not up to any question not pertaining to the exhibits themselves. Angrily Quam turned away and retraced his steps.

Half an hour and many moments of lost temper later, he finally found Juan Zaldivar at the edge of a field, busy adjusting a green-cased farm machine. A relaxed and handsome athlete, now alert and free from the hypnosis of the Starchurch reverie, he flashed his white teeth at Quamodian with an inquiring smile.

"I'm concerned about Molly," Quamodian began.

126

"So am I," Zaldivar nodded quickly. "Her course is dangerous and evil. Yet Almalik forbids any compulsion toward salvation. She must make her own mind up to accept the Visitants . . ."

"No, not that!" cried Andy Quam. "Do you realize she has been very nearly killed by what I suspect is a rogue star?"

Juan Zaldivar looked genuinely shocked. "How terrible!" he cried. "We must do something at once! You must tell her that her one protection is in Almalik. She can delay no longer!"

"No, no," groaned Quamodian. "Listen to me, Zaldivar! It's no longer a matter of just Molly, it's the whole Companionship of the Stars, the universe itself that's threatened. Have you any notion of what a rogue star can do? Look at the sun!"

He gestured at the red and swollen disk, high in the heavens but looking like a stormy dusk. Zaldivar glanced at it through squinted eyes, with an expression of mild inquiry. "Curious," he said, nodding.

"More than curious! Deadly! Dangerous!"

"To Molly?" asked Zaldivar, politely perplexed. "I do not entirely follow you, Monitor Quamodian. But if you are saying now, as you seemed to be denying a moment ago, that Molly is in danger, why, yes, I agree. She is. So are you. So are all who have not accepted the Star, as signified by receiving the Visitants into their bodies."

Andy Quam took a deep breath and controlled himself. The Peace of Almalik, he reminded himself, was a great gift to mankind. Unfortunately those who accepted it—though of course blessed beyond all other men in their health, their joy, their star-given peace—were sometimes hard to deal with, hard to arouse to needed action. But that, of course, was why those like himself, the Monitors and the other free-acting agents of the Star, could not accept the Visitants. He should have known all that; he should have learned to accept it . . .

He said, keeping his temper, "Juan Zaldivar, I ask you to do something for me in the name of Almalik. Since you are in contact with the sentient stars by means of the Visitants, I want you to pass on to them my warning about the creation of the rogue star."

"I have done so," said Zaldivar benignly. "Almalik knows all that I know."

"Good," sighed Andy Quam. He felt a brief relief, a sense of awe at the fleeting vision of all the wisdom and power of the multiple citizen Cygnus, the minds of numberless sentient suns and transcience robots and perfected men knitted together by the fusorian Visitants. "Now," he said, "there's a puzzle you must help me solve. I want to know why that sunbolt struck yesterday. Is Almalik responsible?"

Zaldivar squinted again, then shook his head gravely. "No," he declaimed, "the release of the sunbolt was a violent action. According to our information it destroyed much equipment and contributed to at least one human death. As Almalik is nonviolent, we are clearly not responsible."

Quamodian peered at him. "Was it the rogue that was responsible?"

Juan Zaldivar said serenely, "In that, Monitor Quamodian, we are not concerned. We will not resist."

"But you're in danger! Even the sentient stars are

in danger, if an intellectic creature hostile to them is loose in this galaxy!"

"We will not resist," repeated Juan Zaldivar. "Acting in violence, we should destroy ourselves." And, gently murmuring an apology, he returned to adjust his farm machine.

The boy's message had said he would be at the Zaldivars' home, but he was not in sight. No one was; the dwelling door stood open, but no one answered Andy Quam's call.

There was a crooning, placid, musical drone coming from somewhere above. Quamodian followed the sound, and doors opened before him as the homeostatic dwelling invited him in, up a moving slideramp, to a roof garden.

There sat Deirdre Zaldivar, greeting the morning by playing an instrument which transformed her emotions into art, spinning them into melodious sound, colored form, subtle scent. She greeted him, smiling. Youthful as Molly, her beauty unmarred by the golden star that blazed on her cheek, she was absorbed in her art and reluctant to be disturbed.

"Rufe? Oh, yes, Monitor Quamodian. I know Rufe. But he's not here."

"That's odd, Mrs. Zaldivar," Andy Quam frowned. "He said he'd meet me here. Did he say anything to you?"

Deirdre Zaldivar plucked a strumming chord of sound negligently, watched a pinkish bubble of color grow, turn rose, and then red, then darken into invisibility. "Why, no, Monitor Quamodian. We haven't heard from Rufe, have we?"

She looked inquiringly past Andy Quam. Disconcerted, he turned, and there was the sleek black egg shape of a transcience robot floating over a bed of talisman roses. "Robot Inspector?" he said uncertainly. "I—I didn't notice you were here."

The robot's pulsating plasma oval shimmered brightly. "I am not the robot inspector, Monitor Quamodian," it sang in its high, sweet voice. "That unit is no longer operational. I am its deputy."

"Not operational?"

"It has been disjoined, Monitor Quamodian," hummed the robot placidly. "I have, however, access to all its memory up to the point at which disjunction occurred, so that for all practical purposes you may regard us as the same. Do you wish to employ my services?"

"No," said Andy Quam. "Or—yes. I think so. But I wanted to speak to Mrs. Zaldivar first. Molly has been injured, but she is now resting peacefully. I think she is all right—but in danger, I'm afraid."

Deirdre Zaldivar looked politely concerned. "Too bad," she said regretfully. "She is such a dear girl. But—" she shrugged, smiling at the deputy robot, "she is not yet a member of the Star, of course. Like all nonmembers, she is exposed to the hazards of independent existence." She returned to the console of her instrument and, with a quick run across the keys, built a splendid tower of scent and color and color and sound. "When Molly accepts the Visitants, Monitor Quamodian," she said, watching her composition grow and drift, "everything will be all right. Everything is always all right in the Companionship of the Star."

Andy Quam's exasperation pressure was building

again. He could feel it compressing his brows, grinding his jaws together. He turned to the robot and snapped. "You, then. I want some facts. What happened to the sun?"

"In what respect, Monitor Quamodian?" sang the robot politely.

"Its appearance—look at it! And the plasma bolts it threw at the Earth yesterday. Why?"

"We have no information," reported the robot regretfully.

"Is it true that the multiple citizen Cygnus is not responsible?"

"Quite true, Monitor Quamodian," agreed the robot, its high voice sounding disapproving of the question. "Almalik informs us that this fact was already reported by you to Juan Zaldivar. You are aware that the citizen Cygnus will engage in no violence."

"Then, what about the sun? Has—" the thought suddenly erupted in his mind, almost choking him, "has a rogue intellect been established in this star?"

"The star Sol," sang the robot, "is not a member of the multiple citizen Cygnus, nor has it ever entered into association with any part of the civilized universe. We have no other information about its intellectual status."

"Its abnormal behavior is dangerous to this planet and to all the members of Cygnus on it," protested Andy Quam. "One human being has died already. I fear this danger may extend to the sentient stars of Cygnus."

"Almalik is informed," hummed the robot serenely. "The sentient stars are not alarmed."

131

"*I* am alarmed!" cried Andy Quam. "I require your assistance!"

The robot floated toward him, its plasma oval glowing brightly. "That is your right, Monitor Quamodian," it conceded sweetly. "As long as there is no conflict with the prime directives of Almalik."

"Fine!" snapped Andy Quam. "Begin by informing Almalik of my concern. State that I regard it as absolutely urgent that action be taken!"

"What action, Monitor Quamodian?" asked the robot solicitously.

Quamodian was ready for that. "Request Almalik to review my reports on Solo Scott and on Cliff Hawk's rogue star," he said briskly. "Urge Almalik to contact Clothilde Kwai Kwich. Ask Almalik to suggest alternative routes of additional action."

"But I have done so, Monitor Quamodian," sang the voice of the robot.

"We have no new information about Monitor Kwai Kwich, and no action to suggest!"

Quamodian glared at it furiously. What he might have said next might have cost him lasting regret; but he never had a chance to say it. From down below he heard a high-pitched shout, repeated, calling his name. "Preacher! Preacher, are you there?"

Quamodian sprang to the slideramp, peered down. "Is that you, Rufe?" he called.

The boy appeared, face grimed with tears and sobbing. "Oh, preacher!" he groaned. "It's Miss Zaldivar! She's gone!"

Quamodian's blood seemed to turn cold in his body; time stopped. "Gone? Gone where, boy?"

"I don't know, preacher. I—I think that thing must've come and taken her away!"

The world seemed to turn black around Andy Quam. The boy's voice dissipated like smoke, leaving a thin and fading wisp of terror behind it. Quamodian shuddered, shook himself, tried to think. But thought was beyond him at that moment; he had to act. He grasped the handrail and started to run down the slideramp, against its movement, not waiting for the sensors to detect his presence and respond by reversing the movement of the ramp.

From behind him the voice of the robot, its amplitude raised almost to the point of pain, thundered like the diapason of a giant organ: "Monitor Quamodian, wait! I must ask your intention!"

Quamodian halted, shook himself, half turned, "Intention?" he repeated. "Why—why, I'm going to get her back!"

"In what way, Monitor Quamodian?" roared the robot.

"Why—" Andy Quam thought, then realized he had known the answer all along. "With the Reefer!" he cried. "We're going to hunt that thing down and destroy it!"

The robot's voice, volume somewhat reduced but still an uncomfortable shrill knife edge in the eardrums, trumpeted: "Violence, Monitor Quamodian. You are speaking of violence. The Companions of Almalik cannot support such an expedition!"

"I can!" cried Andy Quam. "I'm a Companion! Our organization exists for this very reason—that we are free to do things for the members of the multiple citizen Cygnus that they are not free to do for themselves."

The robot's black egg floated swiftly toward him. "In the past," it sang, volume reduced almost to normal, whining now, "this was true. But it is known that certain Companions have engaged in undue violence in the name of Almalik. This is a serious error, Monitor Quamodian! In consequence the status of the organization has been reviewed. Although certain freedoms of information and persuasion will remain to the Companions, all use of violence is herefrom prohibited."

Quamodian jumped back in dismay, knocking over a crystal ornament in the shape of a leaping flame; it shattered on the floor, and the robot licked out a flickering tongue of pale plasma to gather up the fragments. "That's impossible!" Quamodian gasped. "We have—we must have freedom to defend the members of the citizen!"

"We do not resist," the robot purred serenely. "That is the prime ethic of the Visitants. The Companions may no longer resist in our name."

Andy Quam hesitated, glanced down at the white, watching face of the boy, kicked a shard of crystal across the room, then abruptly turned and started down the ramp.

"Monitor Quamodian!" sang the robot. "Monitor Quamodian, you have been informed!"

Andy Quam growled wordlessly in his throat and continued. The robot raised its amplitude deafeningly again. "Monitor Quamodian! We demand to know! What is your intention?"

Andy Quam paused just long enough to turn. "What I said!" he shouted defiantly. "I'm going to destroy that thing—with your permission or without it!"

XVIII

In the old Plan of Man cave under the Reefer's hill, the hot bright cloud of plasma had long since dissipated. The womb from which the rogue star had been born was quiet now, no longer fed by the driving energies Cliff Hawk had tapped. But the air still reeked of ionization and burned copper points; the autonomic lighting system flickered unreliably, and the shadows were dark.

Where the great bulk of the sleeth had dropped Molly Zaldivar, the pale cloud of stripped electrons that was the heart of the rogue hung meditatively over her. It had sent the sleeth away; Molly feared it, and something inside the rogue's stored systems recognized that fear. But the girl lay sobbing on the cold concrete of the floor, and some other "instinct" commanded the rogue to make her more comfortable.

Move her. Make her safe, thought the rogue, and hunted among its recently discovered options for a way to do it. At length (some dozens of picoseconds later) it opted for another of its toys, the rusty old handling machine that Hawk had sometimes employed. It was as easy to manipulate as Molly's old electrocar, and slowly and painfully the rogue caused it to crunch on its cleated tracks toward the cave entrance, to come in and approach the recumbent girl.

The operation of the handling machine, easy enough in principle, required a certain continuity of operation to which the rogue was not accustomed; its time-response was creepingly slow, its progress over the rock and rubble of the hillside and cave was intolerable. The rogue rested, drank mass from the air and strength from the stone, then rolled on again.

The girl scrambled to her hands and knees, staring wildly at the clanking machine.

The rogue paused, and tried again its exercises in human language. Speaking through the circuits of the machine's radio, it rasped: "Molly Zaldivar. How can I cause you to love me?"

Molly's eyes widened. "Nightmare!" she cried. "Monster! What are you?"

Painfully the rogue modulated the radio's circuits to reply. "Why am I—a nightmare? Why do you not love me? I—love you, Molly Zaldivar!"

Faintly, far away, it felt that watcher's growing fear.

Despairing, the girl rose, tried to flee; but it was easy for the rogue to reach out with the handling machine's effectors, catch her, and draw her back. She shrieked. The rogue paused, considering. It was difficult to comprehend the processes that affect-ed organized matter. Yet the green radiance that flowed around her was suddenly shot with flashes of red which the rogue recognized as—not "pain," for it had not been able to relate those memories in Cliff Hawk's mind to anything in its own expe-rience; but to a malfunction of some sort, and it was only a step to realize that the malfunction was caused by the harsh grasp of the handling machine on the girl's relatively weak body.

The rogue deposited her as gently as it could on the floor of its cab, and methodically analyzed its findings. It was a long process, requiring more than one microsecond; there was much that it had to deduce or interpolate. Even its own actions were not entirely clear to the rogue; it had no well-formed referent for the term "love," though it had felt quite strongly that this was the proper operator to describe its relationship to Molly Zaldivar. Casually and quickly it detached a section of itself and entered the brain and nervous system of Molly Zaldivar, studying as it went, attempting to sort out the damage that had been done. It seemed quite small, the rogue considered; only a few hundred thousand cells were damaged, and a relatively small proportion of them destroyed. It made a few adjustments which had the effect of stopping the efflux of circulatory fluid, rejoining some separated vessels and ligaments and, contented with its work, exited the girl's body and reassembled itself.

The girl, aware that something was happening but unable to know what, was very close to hysteria. She fumbled about the floor of the cab, pulled herself to the seat, hammered feebly against the windows; orange terror flashed through the radiance that surrounded her, and the sleeth tried to speak to her again:

"Why do you struggle, Molly Zaldivar? Why do you not love me?"

Molly threw herself back on the seat with a ragged laugh. "Love? You can't love!"

"I do love, Molly Zaldivar. Why am I a nightmare?"

She shuddered, forcing herself to speak. "Why? Because you don't have a right to exist, monster! You are a synthetic intellect. The transflection patterns of your mind were created in a cloud of plasma by Cliff Hawk and the Reefer . . ."

When she spoke of Cliff Hawk a golden glow lighted her mind's radiance.

The rogue said: "I am Cliff Hawk."

"You?" The girl caught her breath; she was shaking all over now, half in terror, half in utter uncomprehending bewilderment. "Cliff is dead! I saw him die."

"Yes. Dead. But I am that of Cliff Hawk which survives at all. Cliff Hawk is a member of me. And you must love me."

The girl abandoned herself to a storm of weeping. After some thought, the rogue re-entered her mind, sought for and found certain centers it had learned to recognize and caused her to go to sleep. It then paused and considered what it knew about the maintenance of organic masses of organized matter. This was, in truth, very little; but certain peremptory needs were clear. The girl would need protection against the elements and a place to rest. She would need air for combustion, the rogue thought, and observed that this was in adequate supply from the ambient atmosphere; she would need liquid H_2O, easily procured nearby. And she would also need metabolizable chemicals of the class it described by the vaguely comprehended label "food."

All these matters it determined to deal with. First

it opened the door of its cab. Then it sought out and re-entered the sleeth, hovering half stunned and bewildered over the hilltop, and brought it arrowing swiftly back into the tunnel. The sleeth's great body felt supple and powerful after the clanking paralytic environment of the handling machine; the rogue caused it to soar into the mouth of the tunnel, hurtle down a straightway, round a curve and join the group. It felt joy in the strength of the great muscles, delight in the silent power of its transflection fields, pleasure even in the dreadful radiation that it could evoke from the huge blind eyes. It lifted the girl's sleeping body in the deadly, gentle claws and traced a tightening curve along the tunnel's way, into the mountain and down, until it found a pit that it had not previously observed.

The rogue paused, probing the dark space at the bottom of the pit. It found nothing hostile, nothing of organized organic matter. It was, in fact, a long-forgotten base of the scientific establishment of the Plan of Man; the rogue had no notion what that meant, and still less interest.

Careful with Molly, holding her cuddled against the great sleek belly of the sleeth, it dropped into the dark, drifting slowly downward past the vertical walls, until it dropped out of darkness into a cold, ghostly light. They were in a huge sphere hollowed in the rock at the base of the hill. Once multiplying neutrons had flashed through and saturated a few kilograms of fissionable metal, the nuclear explosion had blossomed and shrugged tens of thousands of tons of rock away, melting the inner shell and holding it suspended, like a balloon, long enough for the dome shape to form. As the pressure leaked away the plastic rock hardened, and what was left was this great ball-shaped cave.

The pale light came from all about it, especially from a pale cold sun of milky mist that hung at the center of the hollow. A spiral staircase, skeletal metal treads and a handrail, wound upward inside a spidery steel tower from the bottom of the globular cavity's floor to a railed platform half inside that high, pale cloud of opal light.

What was the hollow?

What was the light?

The rogue gave those questions no consideration. Tenderly it set Molly Zaldivar down on the bottom of the hollow and allowed her to waken.

To the extent that the nonhuman intelligence of the rogue was capable of satisfaction, it was now pleased with what it had done. It had removed the person of the oddly attractive organized bit of matter called Molly Zaldivar to a place where it would not be harmed by outside activities, and where its own attempts to establish communication could go on without interference. It was a place whose chemistry, pressure and temperature appeared to be compatible with life, as far as the rogue was able to judge.

Of course, the rogue was still comparatively young in time, lacking experience, and even with the absorbed patterns that were all that was left of Cliff Hawk embodied in its own systems, it had no very deep understanding of biological chemistry.

An attractive feature of the cave, for the rogue, was the presence of residual ionizing radiation, coming from the surrounding rock, the very atmosphere inside the bubble, above all from that queerly glowing misty cloud of light. To the rogue this was a welcome source of energy to be tapped at need. It did not know that to Molly Zaldivar it was a death warrant.

When the girl woke up she cried out, peered wildly around the pit, saw the hovering form of the sleeth and tried to leap up and run away. There was nowhere to run. She slipped on the curving stone, black-stained and slick with seeping water, and lay there for a moment, sobbing.

The rogue attempted to form patterns of sound to communicate with her. It was difficult. Even using the transflection fields of the sleeth, modulating them as rapidly and precisely as it could, there was no handy substance for it to vibrate; all it could produce from the shaking of the metallic substance of the nearby tower and steps was a harsh metallic scream, incomprehensible to Molly, and frightening.

The rogue was, for some picoseconds, baffled. Its persona, the sleeth, had no vocal chords, no mechanism at all for making signals in air. But the rogue was more than the sleeth.

It extended a quick plasma finger and probed the tower itself. There, rustless and fresh as the day it was installed, was a bank of instruments; the rogue hunted among them until it found one that possessed a flexible membrane. It spoke through it:

"Molly Zaldivar. You need not be afraid because I love you."

The girl's involuntary scream echoed strangely from the high rounded walls. The rogue floated patiently above her, waiting.

Trembling and unsteady on the slick slope, she

climbed to her feet and stared up at it. With a great effort she whispered, "What are you?"

"Cliff Hawk is a part of me. Call me Cliff Hawk."

"I can't! What sort of monster are you?"

"Monster?" The rogue examined the term carefully, without comprehension. It activated the distant tinny speaker to say: "I am your lover, Molly Zaldivar."

The girl's face wrinkled strangely, but Molly had herself under control now. She smiled, a cold, white and terrible smile, ghastly in that shadowless light. "My lover!" she crooned. She paused in thought. "I am lucky," she said bravely. "What girl ever had so mighty a lover?"

The rogue could not recognize near-hysteria. It was puzzlingly aware that the radiance from the organized matter called Molly Zaldivar was not the gentle, warming glow of rose or pearl that it had wanted to evoke; but it knew far too little of human beings to comprehend what Molly was trying to do. In its sleeth body it dropped gently toward her, meeting her as she rose, and allowed her quivering fingers to stroke the fine, dense fur.

"If I love you," she whispered tremulously, "will you help me?"

Powerful floods of energy thundered through the rogue, mighty and irresistible; it was a species of joy, a sort of elation. The rogue allowed its sleeth body to drop to Molly's feet.

"I'll give you everything," it swore through the distant tinny speaker.

The girl was trembling violently, but allowed the vast black talons to draw her quivering body against the fur. The rogue sensed her terror and tried to reassure her. "We are safe here, Molly Zaldivar. No enemy can reach us."

Her fear did not abate. "I fell in the water," she whispered. "I'm damp and cold . . ."

The rogue made the sleeth's fur warm for her; but still she was afraid.

"I'm a human being," she whimpered. "I'll be hungry. Thirsty. I must have food or I'll die!"

From above them the tinny rattle of the overtaxed speaker shouted: "I'll bring food, Molly Zaldivar! I'll bring all things you need. But we must stay here, where we are safe."

The rogue arranged the pit for her comfort, dried the rock with a searing beam from the sleeth's transflection fields, dragged down a cushion from the tower to make her a resting place. It put her shivering body on it, and reached into her mind to erase her haunting terror.

Presently she slept.

The rogue went foraging in the body of the sleeth. It rose to the top of the pit, squeezed its way through the long passages, climbed into the night. It needed only moments to arrow the score of miles to the nearest human dwelling. It dropped out of the dark onto the little house, crushed a four-legged creature that barked and howled at it, ripped through a wall and seized a refrigerated box filled with human food.

The little box in its talons, it dropped again into the side of the mountain, and paused to consider.

Molly Zaldivar had been in an agony of terror; that much it realized. Why? The rogue, which shared with all intellects the homomorphic trait of considering itself the proper matrix on which all other creatures should be modeled, could not believe that it was its own self which frightened her; no doubt it was its proxy, the sleeth. From the dim stirrings of Cliff Hawk's mind it realized that those great blind eyes, those vengeful talons were likely to be frightening to smaller creatures. It determined to leave the sleeth and visit her in another form.

Under the lip of the cave, where the rogue had abandoned it, the hulk of the robot lay tossed aside. The rogue entered into it, flexed its transcience fields, lifted it into space and, bearing the refrigerated box of food, retraced the long winding route, sank down through the frozen light of that misty opal sun . . .

Molly was awake.

The rogue wearing the egg shaped body of the robot, brought itself up sharply and hung there just out of sight, the food box dangling from its effectors. Molly was no longer stretched out asleep on the cushions it had brought for her. She was in the spidery metal tower, crouched before the bright, ancient control panel, fumbling frantically with the radio. The rogue listened through the ears of the robot:

"Calling Monitor Quamodian!" the girl whimpered. "Oh, please! Andy! Anyone!"

The rogue knew that the radio was dead; it hung there, letting her speak, listening.

"Molly Zaldivar calling Monitor Quamodian! Andy, please listen. I'm trapped in a cave. That thing—the rogue star, whatever it is—has me trapped here, because it says—it says it loves me! And it won't let me go."

Her head fell forward, her hand still on the useless

switch of the radio. She sobbed, "Oh, please help me. It's a hateful, horrible thing—a monster. I—I tried to deceive it, to make it let me go by pretending to—to like it. But it won't . . ."

The rogue, in the persona of the broken transcience robot, sank slowly toward her, burdened with the box of food that it had brought for her. It was struggling in its complex mind with concepts for which it had no names, and little understanding. *Betrayal.*

Anger.

Revenge.

XIX

The Reefer's deep-set eyes glowed like a robot's plasma patch. "Make this thing move, Quamodian!" he roared. "I want that critter for my trophy room!"

Andy Quam hissed in annoyance, "Be still, Reefer! I'm not interested in your game collection. It's Molly Zaldivar's life that concerns me." He bent to the panel of his flyer. He was indeed making it move, as fast as he could, cutting out the autonomic pilot circuits and racing the craft along on manual override. It was a flimsy enough bolt to hurl at a creature that ranked with stars for majesty and might—a simple atomosphere flyer, with a few puny transflection beams that could be used as weapons. But it was all he had.

They arrowed through the chill morning air, along the road toward the misty blue ridge. Over the Reefer's hill a smudge of smoke still lifted and wandered away with the wind. Quamodian's eyes were on it when his transceiver clicked into life. For a moment the speakers hummed and crackled, but there was no voice. Andy Quam scowled with annoyance and leaned to listen.

"What is it?" growled the Reefer, brows knotted under their blond tangle of hair.

"I don't know," said Andy Quam. "Nothing. Listen."

But there was no voice, only the questing carrier sounds. For a moment Andy Quam thought it might have been Molly, and the thought lit his mind with a living image of her red-glinting hair, her haunting oval face, her laughing eyes. But it was not her voice that came from the speaker.

Something was trying to talk to him. An uncanny voice—slow, toneless, laborious. It chilled him with alarm.

"What's that?" demanded the Reefer again. "Quamodian, what are you doing?"

"Be still!" Andy Quam touched the dial, trying to bring the sound in more clearly. It was not a robot's clipped and penetrating whine. It lacked the mechanical precision of an automatic translator. The scattered sounds he made out were not from the universal signal system of the intergalactic society. They were Earth-English. Yet they were somehow alien, monstrously inhuman. It was not a message; it was more like some great, tortured soliloquy, a voice that rambled on and on, brokenly and angrily. The distorted and intermittent signal had no clear message, but it filled Andy Quam with fear.

Climbing slightly, he pushed the flyer to transsonic speed. The narrow black ribbon of road unreeled. Higher hills flashed beneath him. A building flickered. The leaning smudge of smoke was a momentary blur.

Something crept along the road below him.

The Reefer caught Andy Quam's shoulder. "It's that machine!" he bellowed. "An old Plan of Man earthmover—the rogue's using it. Blast it, man! Drive him out into the open!"

Quamodian shrugged the great paw off his arm, and bent to stare down at the road. It was huge and clumsy, lumbering ponderously toward the crest of the ridge on grotesque old caterpillar tracks. It waved claw-ended handling forks around its angular, orange-painted cab.

"Flyer," ordered Andy Quam, "pot that thing for me."

There was a faint deep hiss of departing missiles as the flyer obediently flung out a burst of landing flares at the machine. They were not meant as weapons but would do a weapon's work; they missed, stitching a row of pits across the pavement in front of the machine.

"Sorry, Monitor Quamodian," the flyer apologized mournfully. "I'm not really designed for this sort of work."

"Get its tracks!" Quamodian ordered. "Use all the flares if you have to. Stop it!"

The machine plowed recklessly through the shower of flame. Quamodian spun the flyer around, returned it, passing low over the machine; a new spray of flame darted out toward it, struck it, and clung. The machine slid sidewise, seeming to float on that pool of fire, and Andy Quam saw a broken track flap wildly.

The machine stopped. At a word, the flyer took over automatic control and hovered; the two men looked down.

The machine lay, silent and broken, on the pitted road, while choking fumes rose from the remnants of the flares. Andy Quam turned to the Reefer and demanded, "I've shot it up for you. It doesn't seem to have accomplished a thing. Now what?"

"Now go on!" roared the Reefer. "You've just killed one of the rogue's tools, we haven't touched the beast itself yet. Go on and dig it out!"

Quamodian shrugged, was about to order the flyer on . . .

The klaxon hooted. Red signals blossomed in holographic solidity on the panel. The bubble marker circled a flying object, coming low and fast from the woods behind. It shone with a pale but strange greenish radiation.

"It is the space creature called the sleeth, Monitor Quamodian," reported the flyer. "Indications are that it is under the control of the intellectic being you seek."

The Reefer was briefer and more furious. "That's my critter!" he howled. "Careful! It can eat up a dozen like us any day!"

"Careful!" growled Andreas Quamodian. "Let your animal be careful! Flyer, got any flares left?"

"Two racks, Monitor Quamodian," the machine reported.

"Smash that thing with them!"

The jet leaped away—but, curiously, the flares failed to detonate. Their tracer trails ended in faint red sparks near the oncoming object.

"The sleeth's blanketing them," snarled the Reefer. "You'll have to do better than that!"

"Fire what's left!" shouted Andy Quam, and slapped down the manual override, taking control of the little flyer's transflector beams. He spun them into high, reached out with their pale, deadly fingers toward the sleeth which was growing ever larger before him, the second flight of flares dimming to darkness just like the first.

A sudden lurch threw him against the control panel. "Mal-function, Monitor Qua-modian," the flyer jerked out. "Pow-er fail-ure . . ."

The propulsion field was failing even as the reaching transflection beams were paling and dying. The greenish glow of the sleeth brightened suddenly; the flyer's Klaxon tried to blare, succeeded in rattling a crash alert.

"Hold on!" bawled Quamodian. "We're going to hit . . ."

And they did; they hit hard, the emergency shields failing to function; hard enough to jolt both men like dolls knocked over in a coconut shy. The sleeth soared over them and halted. It was a terrifying sight, horse-sized, catlike, tapered muscles bulging under the sleek black fur. Blazing green, enormous and cold, its eyes bulged blindly out at them.

The Reefer pulled himself together and croaked, "They—they can kill us, Quamodian. Those eyes!"

Quamodian didn't need the warning. There was something in those eyes that was reaching into his mind, freezing his will, icing his spine and muscles. He struggled to make his limbs obey him, and reached for the little hand weapon he kept under the seat of the flyer; but the icy, penetrating numbness had gone too far. He touched the gun, almost caught it, dropped it and sent it skittering across the tipped floor of the flyer; and the sleeth hung there, staring blindly down through the faint shimmer of its trans-flection field, just touching a fallen tree with one horrendous claw . . .

The great blind eyes seemed suddenly smaller. The frightful currents of cold that had drenched Andy Quam's body seemed somehow to recede. He could not move, he was not his own master any longer; but at least, he thought, he was not dying helplessly any more; for some reason the creature had halted the poisonous flow of radiation that had drained the flyer's power banks and nearly drained their lives.

The Reefer gasped hoarsely, "Knew it! Knew it couldn't kill its master." And incredibly, haltingly that big yellow-haired bear of a man was forcing himself to stand erect, lurching with agonizing slowness to the door, dropping to the ground and willing himself to stand erect again, next to the great sleek bulk of the creature from space.

And the forgotten radio speaker of the flyer abruptly rattled harshly and spoke: "Go away, Quamodian. I give you your life—but go!" It was the voice he had heard before, inhuman, unalive, terrifying. Andy Quam fell back, finally drained of the last of his strength. He saw the great talons of the sleeth curve protectingly around the Reefer, clasp him and hold him; saw the great creature surge into the air and away, carrying the Reefer as it disappeared with fantastic speed toward the gap in the hills where the faint smudge of smoke still hung.

And then he felt his flyer rock slightly, twitch, and then slowly and painfully lift itself into the sky. It was not at his order that it flew, but its destination was not in question. It rose to a few hundred feet, turned and headed back for the town.

The hunters had failed. One was now himself a captive, being borne at transsonic speeds toward the cave where the rogue flexed its new powers, practiced at its new repertory of emotions and grew. One was helplessly returning the way he had come. And the girl they had tried to rescue was farther from Andy Quam's help than the farthest star.

Of one thing he was sure: he had been defeated. His mere human strength had not even sufficed to get him past the rogue's puppet, the sleeth. He would have no chance against the might of the rogue itself.

XX

The rogue, wearing the borrowed body of the robot inspector, sank slowly through the cold opal light of the great bubble under the earth. The refrigerated box of food, held lightly in its transflection fields, seemed suddenly too heavy to carry, and the rogue let it drop.

It crashed to the seep-stained floor in a thunder that rolled around the cavern, split open, spilling out the little parcels of human food. The noise startled Molly Zaldivar. She looked up at the robot form, her face shocked and hollowed in that icy, lifeless light. A scream blazed through the echoing thunder.

For a moment, seeing the gleaming black egg-shaped body of the robot settling toward her, Molly had the wild hope that it was the familiar robot inspector from the Starchurch, somehow come to rescue her, perhaps with Andy Quam right behind. But the hope did not last long enough to survive the terror in her face. She got up stiffly, abandoning the useless radio, and climbed slowly down the spiral steps toward the bottom of the rock bubble.

The sweet high voice of the robot, modulated by the unpracticed mind of the rogue, spoke to her:

"Molly Zaldivar. Why did you speak falsely to me?"

She did not answer. There was a pause, while the rogue pondered its conflicting impulses. "I will not harm you," it droned at last. "You need not be afraid—because I love you, Molly Zaldivar."

Her face twisted and she lifted her hands to the floating robot. "If you love me, won't you let me go?" she cried.

"Because I love you—I can never let you go."

She shouted with all her strength, "Then I hate you, monster!" Her voice was hoarse and despairing; despairing, too, was the angry green radiance that surrounded her in the sight of the rogue, colors and patterns that spoke to him of fury. It left her standing there and soared away, wheeling around the spidery tower. Suddenly it felt the clothing of the robot that it wore confining; it slipped out, left the robot hanging mindlessly on its transflection fields and, once more a nearly invisible cloud of stripped electrons, perched on the metal rails just below the pale, milky mist of light that hung in the center of the sphere.

It spoke to her through the robot: "Molly Zaldivar, I am strong and you are weak. Your hatred cannot harm me. True?"

She shook her head without words, utterly weary.

"But I will not harm you—if I can avoid it, Molly Zaldivar. We will stay here—until you love me."

"Then I'll die here," she said tonelessly.

The rogue pondered the problem for many nanoseconds. It said at last, "Then I shall absorb you as you die. You will be a member of me, like Cliff Hawk."

The girl said, weakly, fearfully, then with gathering rage, "Oh, please—you mustn't! You say you love me—heaven knows what you mean by that— but if it means anything at all to you, you must let me go."

"Never, Molly Zaldivar."

"You can't keep me!".

"I can, Molly Zaldivar. I am stronger than you."

She shrieked, "But there are things which are stronger! Almalik! Almalik is stronger than you. And he will find you yet, even hiding here."

The rogue searched its memory patterns for a referent for the term "Almalik." Almost hesitantly it said, "What is 'Almalik'?"

"Almalik is the spokesman star for Cygnus. Almalik commands multitudes—fusorians and men, robots and stars. His multitudes will find you, here or anywhere. And even if you were as strong as Almalik, you are all alone while he has legions!"

The rogue's plasma rippled in thought. "I have met Almalik's robot," it said at last. "It is now a member of me."

"One robot! Almalik owns many millions."

The rogue did not reply. Thoughtfully it clung to the metallic rail of the cryptic old device, studying the girl. She was exhausted now, the green fire of her fury dying, waiting for a move from the rogue.

To the rogue, painfully learning the uses of those human qualities called emotions, Molly Zaldivar was a most confusing stimulus. There was enough of the residual identity of Cliff Hawk in the rogue to give force and direction to its feelings about Molly; it possessed attitude sets which could have been called "pity" or "love." The rogue recognized that the girl was small, and weak, and mortal, and afraid; it even felt some sort of impulse to ease her wild terror, heal her pain and rage. It simply had no effectors capable of the job.

At the same time it recognized that in a sense she represented a threat. The polarization of the other human, Andreas Quamodian, toward her was certain to produce an attempt on his part to interfere again. The rogue did not estimate that the attempt would be successful, but it might be an annoyance; and it took the precaution of detaching some part of its attention to invest its creatures, the sleeth and the handling machine, deploying them as scouts between Wisdom Creek and the mountains.

But there were puzzles the rogue could not solve.

The answers to some of them were far from this cave. It detached itself from its high iron perch in the opal mist and left the girl, watching and trembling.

The rogue sent its awareness out into the universe. It sensed the tangle of dark hills above the bubble cave, stretched, expanded and encompassed cubic miles of space with its consciousness. It observed the bright anger and fear of the human creatures from whom it had stolen the box of food, studied the sleeping presence of Andreas Quamodian, observed the deployment of its own tools, the sleeth and the machine; and it reached farther still.

It reached out until it grasped the roundness of the planet Earth, turning between its bare moon and the red, swelling sun, the sun that had struck at the rogue in those first moments of its existence.

The star was still angry, still roiled and troubled. The rogue studied it carefully, but avoided reaching out to it; it had not been harmed by that triple bolt of energy that had been the sun's riposte, yet did not consider it advisable to provoke another.

The rogue expanded again, reached out its perceptions to the stars. It found them to be suns like this sun, single, coupled, multiple, burning all across the dust and darkness of the galaxy—some tinier than Earth's cold moon, some mightier than Earth's sullen sun. Even beyond the stars it peered, to find a bleak and empty vastness of infinite space and cruel cold. Then in the eternal floods of blackness it perceived the glowing, tiny lights of other galaxies. Ill-informed and unfearing, the rogue studied the numbers and varieties of galaxies. Faintly, it sensed the place of that watching being, still beyond its reach. It returned to nearer stars.

Almalik.

It was time for the rogue to probe into the meaning of the term "Almalik."

There was no problem in finding Almalik; in the captured impulses of the robot inspector was a clear understanding of where Almalik lay in space, and the rogue turned its attention there.

And there was the might of Almalik, the splendor of his thirteen suns, all greater than the small Earth star that had tried to destroy the rogue. It counted them, studied their spin, tested the energies they hurled into the void. Six splendid double stars arranged in hierarchically greater doubles; one single sun with many wheeling planets. The thirteen suns radiated many colors in the optical bands of energies, but the rogue also saw that they shared a common golden glow of unity . . .

And Almalik felt the rogue's fleeting touch.

Hello, little one.

Almalik did not speak. Least of all did he speak in words; but he sent a signal which was at once greeting and wry pity. The signal was powerful but soundless, serene and slow.

The rogue listened impassively, waiting for more.

Little one, we have been looking for you. The silent voice was mightier than thunder, gentle as— what? The rogue had only an imperfect analogy: gentle as love. *We have received information about you. You have destroyed patterns we cherish. You have damaged entities who were part of us. Little one, what do you wish?*

The rogue considered the question for some time.

It framed an answer with difficulty: *Knowledge. Experience.* And then, after a pause, it added, *Everything.*

The multiple suns of Almalik glowed serenely golden; it was almost like a smile. From behind the round Earth, behind the many thousand stars and dust clouds, the signal came: *Knowledge you may have. Ask a question.*

The rogue asked it at once: *Why will you destroy me?*

The soundless voice was cool, aloof, immeasurably sure. *Little one, we cannot destroy you or any sentient thing.*

Green anger filled the rogue. It was a contradiction, Almalik's statement opposed to Molly Zaldivar's. It had not known of the existence of lies until Molly Zaldivar told it she loved it, then showed she did not. Now it knew of lies, but little of mortal error; the contradiction seemed to mean a lie, a lie meant enmity. Red hatred froze the rogue: sudden fury shook its plasma violently.

It dropped from its great, tenuous vantage point, contracted to a swirl of luminescence, and sank back into the mountain just as the planet was turning that part of its surface to the angry rising sun. The splendid suns of Almalik were gone. For a while.

The rogue floated down to Molly Zaldivar. In the high, singing voice of the robot it cried: "We are leaving this place. Almalik has lied to me. I hate him now."

She lay spent and shuddering on the torn cushions, staring at the rogue.

It said: "I hate Almalik. Almalik thinks me small

and helpless, and will destroy me if he can. But I am growing, I will grow still more, I will grow until I am mightier than Almalik."

White and haggard in the dead opal light from the ancient cloud, the girl's face had no expression. She lay hopeless and uncaring, waiting for what the rogue had to say.

"I shall destroy Almalik," it sang in the robot's clear whine. "Then you will love me, Molly Zaldivar, or I will destroy you too."

XXI

Andy Quam landed his flyer before the control dome of the transflex cube and grated, "Control dome! Connect me direct with Headquarters of the Companions of the Star, Almalik Three!"

"Your authorization, sir?" the control dome inquired politely.

"Fully authorized! Highest priority!"

"One moment, sir," the control dome said doubtfully. But it did not refuse him. In a moment it said, "I am seeking your circuits, sir. There is a 200-second delay now estimated; will you wait?"

"You bet I'll wait," growled Andy Quam, and sank dourly back in his seat. He ached. Battling rogue stars and strange beings and men from space was not the kind of life he was used to. But if it was what he had to do to save Molly Zaldivar, he would *get* used to it!

A small figure appeared at the corner of the square, running hard toward him. Tiny spurts of dust flowered at his heels, and he was gasping as he reached the flyer. "Preacher!" Rufe gasped. "What happened? How's Molly Zaldivar?"

"She's still in the cave," said Quamodian shortly. "I think. Anyway, I never saw her."

"Then what—what are you going to do?"

"Wait." But they didn't have to wait long. The speaker clicked and hummed, and a sweet nonhuman voice sang:

"Companions of the Star, Chief Warden of Monitors speaking. How may I serve you?"

"You can serve me best," said Andy Quam belligerently, "by getting an emergency survey team out here on the double! This is Monitor Andreas Quamodian speaking. I request—no, cancel that. I *demand* immediate action!"

The sweet high voice sang sorrowfully, "Ah, Monitor Quamodian. We have been advised of your statements and actions."

"Ha!" barked Andy Quam. "Of course you have! You've been told of my report that a created intellect in the form of a rogue star is loose here; that I have requested authority to use force against it; that I have stated that certain humans and nonhuman intellects have been damaged, destroyed or threatened by it. And you've ignored what I said."

"Unfortunately, Monitor Quamodian, we have seen no reason to accept this report."

"You think I'm wrong, eh?"

"Not 'wrong,' Monitor Quamodian. It is merely

that we do not assess the same quantitative need for action."

"I see," snapped Andy Quam. "Then look at it this way. I report that a Monitor of the Companions of the Star is suffering paranoid delusions; that he believes himself and his friends attacked by monsters; that in his insanity he is capable of wildly destructive acts of violence; and that this will inevitably reflect great discredit to all Monitors. What quantitative assessment do you give *that?*"

"Why—why, Monitor Quamodian, that's frightful! We'll send a survey team at once. Who is this deranged monitor?"

"Me!" snapped Andy Quam, and severed the connection.

They left the flyer grumbling to itself in the middle of the square before the transflex gate. "Stupid thing to do," it was saying resentfully. "They'll take you off the roll of Monitors sure. Then what will become of me? Some menial job ferrying tourists ..."

The boy's house was only minutes away, and there Andy Quam showered, ate, drank thirstily of the cold, rich milk the kitchen machines produced for him. He braced himself for the arrival of the emergency survey team. "How long, preacher?" the boy demanded. "How long before they get here?"

Quamodian considered. "Twenty minutes to think things over. Half an hour to assemble a team. Ten minutes to get their transflex priorities approved—a few seconds to travel. I'd call it an hour."

"Gee! Why, that's only twenty minutes from now. Just think, in twenty minutes I'll be seeing all those crazy three-headed beings, and green-shelled beetles, and . . ."

"We do not comment on the physical peculiarities of any citizen," Andy Quam said firmly. "Didn't your parents teach you that?"

"Well, yes," the boy admitted.

"Come to think of it," Quamodian went on, "where are your parents? Aren't they ever home?"

The boy shuffled his feet. "Sure, preacher. They're just, uh, busy."

"Rufe!"

"Yes, preacher?" His face was angelically innocent.

"Rufe, let's cut out the nonsense. You're hiding something. I can't imagine what, or why—but let's have it!"

"Aw, preacher. It's nothing. It's—" he looked up at Andreas Quamodian anxiously. Quamodian gazed implacably back. "Well," said the boy, "it's just that they were acting a little funny. They've gone off in a flyer to Nuevo York."

"Nuevo York! Why, that's two thousand miles away!"

"A little more, preacher. Figured it'd take them a day or two each way."

"Why?"

"Well, that's the part that's kind of funny. I mean—gee, preacher, there's nothing wrong with my parents! They're not crazy or anything. They just, well, said the same kind of thing you were saying. About some sort of rogue intellect loose on the earth, and the robot inspector here wouldn't listen to them and they didn't have the right of direct contact with Almalik, like you. So they figured they'd better report it to Nuevo York, where people might be more interested."

Quamodian sat up alertly. "You're still hiding something," he accused. "Why would you be ashamed of their knowing about the rogue star? It's true, you know."

"Sure, preacher. Only . . ."

"Only what?"

The boy flushed. "It's just that they were talking about it two days ago. That's when they left."

Quam said, "But that can't be! The rogue star wasn't even created then! Oh, I see!"

The boy nodded unhappily. "That's the part that's got me a little mixed up, preacher. They thought there was one when there *wasn't*."

They were back at the transflex cube with minutes to spare, but the emergency survey team was early. Evidently they had wasted no time. The control dome cried, through Quamodian's flyer radio: "Stand back! Keep the area clear for a party from Almalik Three, now arriving!"

"Gosh!" whispered Rufe. His eyes were round as Saturn's rings, his worries about his parents temporarily out of his mind. "Where are they, preacher? Shouldn't they be coming through? What's keeping them? *Oh*."

A dozen grass-green spiral beings, like tiny coils of springs, emerged from the cube. They were twisting in orbit around each other, approaching the man and the boy with a whistle of high-frequency sound. "What in tarnation is that, preacher?" demanded the boy.

"It is not courteous to stare. I don't recognize the species; a multiple citizen of some kind."

"And that! And—oh, gosh, look at that one!"

"All citizens, I'm sure." But even Quamodian drew his breath sharply, as from behind a foamy, almost translucent bubble of pink there appeared the shark's fangs and slitted eyes of a citizen of clearly carnivorous ancestry. The rest of the citizen was no improvement; it loped on enormously powerful clawed legs like a kangaroo's, possessed two pairs of upper limbs that seemed boneless and lithe as an elephant's trunk, terminating in vivid blue manipulating organs that were almost the duplicate of the snout of a star-nosed mole.

But the fourth member of the group, and the one who advanced on Andy Quam, looked human in a way that made him stare. She wore the garb of a somewhat too sophisticated galactic citizen, her face made up beyond the point of recognition, her dark hair piled into a perfumed tower. But change her clothes and makeup, he thought, put a simple dress of Molly's on her instead of the mirror-bright tights, the fluffed bodice and shoulders, the painted diamonds of bare skin; scrub her face of the two-inch angled eyebrows and the bright blue eye shadow and rouge—and she would be a perfect duplicate of Molly Zaldivar.

Striding toward him, she abruptly stopped. Her shadowed eyes flew wide, like a startled doll's. A crimson flush showed around the edges of her makeup. Her bright lips parted as if gasping, "Andy!" But no sound came. Slowly the exposed patches of skin drained chalk-white. At last she tossed her tall coiffure and swept on toward him.

"Monitor Quamodian—" momentarily, her voice held a breathless quiver. "If you really don't recognize me, I'm Senior Monitor Clothilde Kwai Kwich. You may be interested to know that I was able to return with my subordinates to Companion Headquarters, where we have begun a new analysis of our collected data on rogue stars."

Andy Quam swallowed twice. He wiped the palm of his hand on his tunic and extended it for shaking.

"I'm delighted that you got away," he bubbled breathlessly. "I've been trying to learn what happened, but nobody would tell me anything . . ."

"Never mind the small talk," she snapped. "Please speak briefly and responsively, when it is necessary for you to speak at all. Your idiotic meddling here has forced me to leave more interesting work at headquarters. I'm assigned to clean up the mess you've made. What the devil are you up to now?"

Quamodian stiffened resentfully. "I'm not meddling . . ."

"The traffic safety inspectors say you are," she cut him sharply off. "If you want it explained in baby talk, the rogue star that Cliff Hawk contacted is trying to protect the infant rogue from your officious interference. That's why it sent Solomon Scott to keep you from coming to Earth. That's why it trapped you on its own planet. The inspectors predict that it will be forced to take additional action, unless you restrain yourself."

She gave him no time to inquire what that additional action might be.

"These other citizens and I have little time to waste. We wish to use it effectively. I suppose our best first move is to make an on-site investigation of the totally needless events that your stupidity have brought about."

"I had nothing to do with what has happened here." Flushing, Andy Quam dropped his unshaken hand. "Why, I couldn't even get out of town . . ."

"Let's get moving." She ignored his feeble protest. "My associates can provide their own transport, but I require a vehicle."

"Of course." Helplessly, he shrugged. "Here's my flyer."

Without a word, Senior Monitor Clothilde Kwai Kwich brushed past him to enter the flyer. Dazed, Andy Quam turned to follow. The boy caught his arm.

"Say, preacher," he hissed furiously. "What the dickens is the matter with you?"

"I don't know." He shook his head unhappily. "I'm sure I don't know."

After a moment he followed the girl into the flyer.

XXII

The rogue was much larger now, and wiser, and stronger. It sensed that far watcher's anxious observation, but it wanted no defense.

It did not seem much different to the despairing eyes of Molly Zaldivar, for at best it was only a cloud of stripped surging electrons, a controlled violence of particles that would have been her death if the rogue's own energies had not kept its components bound to its central mass. But it had fed and grown. It had assimilated neural reactions from Cliff Hawk, the robot, the sleeth, the hundred living creatures larger than microorganisms that it had absorbed into itself. It was by no means finished with either growing or learning. Perhaps it was almost mature in size and strength and intelligence. Far from mature however, in its understanding of itself.

Molly made no sound as the radiant whirl summoned the sleeth to it, and entered into the black terrifying shape of the predator from space. The sleeth dropped down upon her and caught her, coldly but harmlessly, in its razored talons, now sheathed in their armored cases. It rose with her through the center of the globe, flew through the cold core of that edgeless opal glow and on and out, tracing the endless passageways to the surface.

Molly did not stir. She was past fear or worry; she was not resigned, but she was passive.

She would not have struggled even if she had known how close to death that murderous opal glow had brought her. But she did not know.

She did not respond even in the hues of emotion by which the rogue interpreted her mental state. No green blaze of hate, no blues or violets of fear. No spark of love; emotion had left her, leaving her dark, and empty, and merely waiting.

Bearing Molly Zaldivar in the bubble of atmosphere trapped in the sleeth's transflexion fields, the rogue left the round Earth.

Tardily they dawdled through the "thick" gases that were the solar atmosphere—so tenuous at one A.U. that human instruments could barely record them, and human bodies would have burst and foamed; but still too thick for the sort of speeds that the sleeth, commanded and driven by the starlike energies of the rogue, could develop. Even so, in minutes they were past gassy Jupiter and Saturn; the void was more nearly empty now, and the rogue drove the sleeth more fiercely.

So fiercely that time seemed to stop.

These were not physical energies that the rogue commanded now; they were the transflexion fields of the sleeth and itself. They leaped through empty spaces, through folded light and darkness, through bitter cold and twisting force and giddy deeps of vastness, leaped to the golden suns of Almalik . . .

And were there.

A thin sighing shout whispered passionately in the ears of Molly Zaldivar:

"Observe!" it shrieked, almost soundlessly. "I have begun to destroy Almalik!"

"You cannot," she said bleakly.

"Observe!" it shrieked again, and subsided. It was the molecules of atmosphere itself that the rogue was shaking now, to make sounds that the girl could hear. It could produce little volume, but in the girl's tiny bubble of air, gazing at the twelve bright but distant stars and one nearby the blinding sun that was Almalik, in the middle of the awful soundlessness of interstellar space, there was no other sound loud enough to drown it out, nothing but her own heart and breath and the faint mindless singing of the sleeth.

"I begin!" whispered the tiny scream, and like a

hawk stooping to its prey the rogue drove them toward the nearest planet.

It was a small world, less than Pluto and farther from its primary; the horizon was strangely rounded, the surface mottled with creeping blobs of liquid gas.

With a power summoned from its infinite reserves, the rogue seized it, entered it—became it. It grew once more. It fed quickly and avidly, seized new atoms, sucked electrons into the spreading patterns of its being, took new energies from frozen stone. It reached out to survey the space around itself, found ions, gas molecules, a hurtling moonlet—and farther off, a small metal mass inhabited by organic masses of organized matter. The rogue did not know it was a spaceship; did not care.

It drew the spaceship and the sleeth at once to itself. The ship crashed bruisingly on the surface of the tiny world. With the sleeth it was more gentle, but not gentle enough. The creature struck against a spire of frozen hydrates, screamed soundlessly and went limp. And as it lost control, with it went the bubble of air it carried in its transflexion fields, and Molly Zaldivar lay open to the murderous empty cold of space.

For many nanoseconds the rogue considered what it had done. As best it knew how to be so, it was alarmed.

At length it seized upon a buried shelf of rock beneath the frozen gases and shook it to make words. "Molly Zaldivar!" rumbled the planet. "What is happening to you?"

The girl did not answer. She lay cradled in a bed of the planet's—of the rogue's own, now—crystal snow, beside the crumpled black body of the sleeth. She did not breathe; there was no longer any air for her to breathe. Dark blood frothed and froze on her face.

"Molly Zaldivar!" groaned the rock of the planet's crust. "Answer!"

But there was no answer.

The rogue tested its powers, felt their new magnitude. Now it was a planet, its coat of frozen gas a skin, its cragged granite mountains the bones, its deep pools of cooling magma a heart of sorts. The rogue was not used to so large a body. It regretted (insofar as it understood regret) that its body was unkind to Molly Zaldivar, too airless, too cruelly cold.

From the wreckage of the spaceship organized masses of organic matter were exiting, clad in metallic artificial skins. The rogue did not recognize that they were citizens who might be of help to Molly Zaldivar; it reached out a thoughtless effector and slew them. And then it again practiced the sensation it experienced as regret; for it realized that they had owned supplies of water and air, warmth and pressure that could have been used for Molly Zaldivar.

No matter. The rogue was now the planet, and could dispose the planet's resources. It would not let her die.

It shielded her from cold, warmed the frozen gas around her and cupped it in a sphere of transflexion forces. With bits of matter taken from the creatures it had destroyed it healed the damage to her lungs. It warmed her stiffened body, helped her breathe again, found the spark of life in her . . .

And the girl stirred and spoke.

169

"What are you doing, monster?" she moaned.

"I am saving your life, Molly Zaldivar," rumbled the rocks. "I am destroying Almalik!"

"You cannot, monster," sobbed the girl.

"Observe!"

The rogue's transflection field was vaster now, spreading to hold all its continents of dark and ancient rock, its seas of snow, to contain all its great mass.

With all its might, the rogue prepared to strike at Almalik.

It halted the planet in its orbit and turned inward toward that white and splendid single sun, the brightest star of Almalik.

And in its hate for Almalik it drove inward, toward collision with the star.

The sleeth was cruelly hurt; but the creature that had evolved to kill pyropods in space was not easily killed. It stirred. The great empty eyes gazed into space, then bent to look into the eyes of Molly Zaldivar. Ripples of muscle pulsed under the dark, hard flesh. It's transflection fields grew again; it lifted lightly from the frozen gas on which it lay, and its high singing sound grew in volume. The sleeth was not an intelligent creature as man is intelligent, or the other citizens of the galaxies; but it had awareness. It recognized that something had owned it for a time; it felt that the something was gone, now that the rogue had retreated to explore its new planetary body. It remembered Molly Zaldivar . . .

And when the rogue next turned its attention to the girl she was gone.

The rogue was quick to search for her, and find her. She was in flight.

Mounted on the sleek black shoulders of the sleeth, veiled in its transflection fields, she was climbing away from the rogue planet's frigid skin of snow, flying toward the inner planets of that great white star toward which the planet was plunging.

The rogue thrust out a darting arm of plasma, of its own electrons meshed in transcience forces. It reached to overtake her, pierced effortlessly the sleeth's transflection shield, shook her small sphere of air with an effector.

"Where are you going, Molly Zaldivar?" the air screamed shrilly in her ear.

She turned her head to look at the rogue's shining plasma finger, but she did not answer. The rogue paused, considering. There was strangeness here. Strange that to the rogue she seemed so very lovely. The redder suns of Almalik struck red fire from her hair; the blue suns burned violet in her eyes. But why should these things matter? the rogue asked itself, interested and curious. Why should the remembered and absorbed thought patterns of the organized matter called Cliff Hawk exert so powerful an influence on it still? The rogue made the air shriek in a piercing whisper again: "I love you, Molly Zaldivar. Once I was tinier than you, so small you could not see me; now I am so huge you are no more than a fleck of dust. We have never been akin, and I see no bridge for love between us—but I love you!"

"You're insane, monster," she said at last. But her eyes were gentle.

The rogue pondered. "Where are you going?" it demanded again.

"I am flying to the inhabited planets of Almalik. On Kaymak they will deal with you—once I warn them."

"Do you hate me, Molly Zaldivar?"

The girl frowned at its bright sensor and shook her head. "You can't help what you are."

The rogue scanned all her matter for the cold green blaze of fury; it was absent. Eagerly it asked, "Then do you love me now?"

Her face crinkled oddly about the eyes, the skin tawny gold beneath Almalik's far suns. "How could I? I am human—you a monster!" And her violet eyes were damp as they peered at the rogue's shining sensor.

"I love you . . ."

"Insane!" sobbed the girl. And then, "Perhaps I pity you, because you are so sadly deformed, because all your power is thrown away." She shook her head vigorously, the colored lights of Almalik dancing in her hair. "I'm sorry for you!"

She paused, then said, "If I am in love, I think it must be with little Andy Quam. Monster, I will go back to him. Once I get to the inhabited planets and give my warning—and you are destroyed—I will go to him through a transflex station. But I pity you, monster."

"I will not be destroyed."

"You will be destroyed—unless you kill me first, and keep me from warning the inhabited worlds."

The rogue thought for microseconds. Then at last it shook the air again. "I will not destroy you," the air shrieked. "But I will not be destroyed. Observe!

172

I will kill Almalik before you can warn anyone!"

And it withdrew its plasma arm, as the girl stared wonderingly after.

The rogue flexed its energies, and prepared for the assault.

It tightened the transflection fields that held and moved its planetary mass. The agonized rock of its mantle screamed and grated as it flattened its bare black peaks, compressed its deserts of snow, squeezing itself into a denser projectile. It drove itself toward the blazing sun.

I will die, thought the rogue. *So will Almalik.*

Tardily, almost carelessly, the congeries of massed beings that made up the total of Almalik took note of the intruder and lifted a careless effector to defend itself.

It was not the white star ahead of the rogue that resisted. That sun lay steadily glowing, ignoring the threat. But from a mighty double sun above it, a golden giant and its immense blue companion spinning close together, a bolt was launched.

The bolt sprang from the inner plasmas of the golden star, and its energies were immense. An enormous leaping snake, thicker than the rogue's own snow-encrusted planetary body, blazed bright as the star itself. It flashed with transflection speed across the void, faster than the rogue could move to evade it.

But it bypassed the rogue, and struck toward Molly Zaldivar.

Even at the planetary distances that already separated them, the rogue could see the red flash of terror dart through her being as she saw that darting coil of golden fire. *Help me, monster!* she cried; the rogue could hear no words, but the message was clear, and it responded.

It hurled out an arm of its own ions and their linking transcience energies, coiling it into a plasma shield around the girl and the sleeth. But it was not strong enough. The golden arm of Almalik was stronger; it burst through the shielding plasma wall, coiled a net of golden fire around Molly and the sleeth and snatched them away toward that double sun.

The rogue could not help her. But an emotion that it could not identify as savage joy filled all its patterned mass. *She called me. She asked my help. If I cannot help her, I still can destroy this near white star of Almalik!*

The rogue paused, testing itself, preparing itself to dispose of energies greater than even it had yet employed. It was not strong enough, it calculated coldly. Not yet. It needed to be stronger.

The planet was cold, but at its core it was not yet dead; crushed gelid masses of iron and heavier metals still seethed, not yet congealed into solids, not yet exhausted of radioactivity and heat. From them the rogue devoured energy and strength. Controlled lightnings flashed along its plasma paths. The planetary mass of its body was now no more than a slinger's pebble to it; a weapon, a missile, a way of killing Almalik.

The rogue intensified its driving field until its crushed mountain ranges smoked, and the deserts of snow thawed and bubbled into boiling seas. The deep core shuddered with earthquake shocks; arcs and auroras raged through its reborn air.

The rogue plunged on to shatter the enemy star.

But Almalik was not unprepared.

From the binary sun above, the golden spear of plasma stabbed at the rogue again. It pierced all the shielding fields, burned through its steaming seas exploded its crust and jarred its heart with seismic waves. The rogue coldly calculated its damage. *Much. Not too much. I still can kill Almalik!*

The plasma snake recoiled to strike again, and yet again, pocking all the rogue's surface with enormous glowing craters, shattering its being with waves of destruction that the rogue felt as searing pain.

But the rogue would not let itself be destroyed.

It drew on its last immense reserves to increase the power of its transflection shields, holding all the atoms of its shattered planetary mass in a remorseless, destroying grip. Daring—and learning—it even reached out to suck new energies from the plasma snake itself.

Molly Zaldivar and the sleeth were gone now, lost even to the rogue's far-ranging perceptions as the plasma coil drew them back toward some distant planet's surface. Every bit of matter of more than molecular dimensions for many A.U.'s around was gone, drawn into the rogue itself or volatilized by the seething energies employed.

But the rogue was not destroyed. It plunged on to strike the unresisting white sun. It knew the watcher's pride in its wild rebel power, and they both rejoiced.

XXIII

"Monitor Quamodian," said the flyer chattily, "You're not going to hear much with your bare ears. They're talking about you."

Quam glanced at Monitor Clothilde Kwai Kwich, who was inspecting the fittings of the flyer with distaste, and apparently whispering to herself. "I don't know if I want to hear," he muttered.

The girl said aloud, without looking at him, "What you want makes little difference, Monitor Quamodian. There will no doubt be times when the other citizens will have inquiries to direct to you, or instructions. I do not wish to be distracted by relaying messages, therefore equip yourself with proper hearing facilities."

Andy Quam grumbled, but accepted the tiny earpiece the flyer offered him on an effector. "... flimsy old wreck," a shrill voice was piping in his ear as he put it on. "We will follow, but kindly move as rapidly as you can." The voice had an odd humming, almost echoing quality, as though a well-trained chorus were speaking in almost perfect unison. Quamodian guessed it was the multiple citizen of green spirals.

He disregarded them, quickly inspected his flyer. Its homeostatic devices had repaired the damage, restored the racks of flares. Not that they would be needed, he hoped. Or would be of any use if they were. But they were better than nothing.

"We're all set," he announced. "I guess."

Monitor Kwai Kwich said, with offensive patience, "Then can we not begin?"

Quamodian hunched grimly over the controls and ordered the flyer into the air. The sun was in his eyes as they spun and rose. Nearly doubled in diameter, its red disk was now so dull that his naked eyes could watch it without discomfort. Dark splotches marred it. He thought of saying something to the girl, but decided against it—although she, a stranger here, might not realize there was anything odd about its appearance. Let her find out, he thought. It didn't matter anyway. All that mattered was that he now had help—a kind of help—against the rogue.

They arrowed south across the narrow lake and the first dark foothills, the multiple green citizen and the pinkly glowing cloud following effortlessly behind. The predator citizen with the enormous fangs lolled silently on the padded seats behind Andy Quam and the girl, while Rufe sat on the floor beneath it, looking apprehensively at its teeth. There was a continuing buzz of conversation on the transcience bands coming through his earpiece, but Quamodian disregarded it. He was not interested in their opinions of his flyer, himself, or the planet that had spawned humanity. All he wanted from them was their help.

It was dark as they reached the hill that held the cave; the sun was still some distance above the horizon, but its dulled rays gave only a looming twilight in the sky, very little on the ground about the cave mouth. He circled the dark mouth of the cave, searching for the sleeth or any hostile thing. There was nothing. All the landscape held that ominous tinge of red, but nothing moved on it.

Flying warily, he approached the rubble of the demolished door.

"Deserted," sang the tiny chorus of the grass-green spirals. "We detect nothing. Another entrance exists lower down."

Senior Monitor Clothilde Kwai Kwich glanced hesitantly at Andy Quam. "There is a good deal of destruction here," she admitted.

"I told you!"

"Yes. Perhaps there has been an error."

"Lower down!" chanted the spirals. "Other indications! Worth investigating!" And the soft whisper of the cottony pink cloud citizen sighed:

"Forces have been deployed in the lower area of considerable magnitude. Forces still exist in being of unusual characteristics."

Senior Monitor Kwai Kwich said, almost apologetically, "We should investigate."

"Right," rasped Quamodian, and sent the flyer spinning down around the mountain, searching for the lower entrance. The pink cloud citizen was there before him, hovering like a puff of steam at the spout of a kettle before the tunnel mouth.

"You lead," it sighed. "Dispersed matter like myself may be vulnerable."

But Quamodian had not waited for permission. He thrust the flyer into the tight throat of the tunnel, probing with its searchlights for the sleeth, for Molly Zaldivar, for any trace. All he found was the tightening spiral passage itself, lined with evidences of destruction. "Forces of great magnitude," chanted the spirals, whirling about a burst wall, a ripped stanchion. "Evidence of transflection energies. Evidence of plasma activity."

Rufe, forgetting his fear of the long-toothed citizen behind him, stood leaning over Quamodian's shoulder. "Gee, preacher," he whispered, thrilled. "Look at that! Something really racked this place up!"

There was no doubt about that. Staring about as the flyer slid smoothly forward on its transflection fields, Quamodian saw that what had happened in this tiny enclosed space had involved more than merely chemical energies. For the first time he really understood what was meant by a "rogue star;" tiny though the creature had been, less than a gram in weight at first, it had commanded forces capable of thrusting steel and rock out of its way like tissue.

The long-snouted predator citizen lifted its muzzle and howled a sentence; the translator in Quamodian's ear rendered it as: "Be careful! Monitor Kwai Kwich, should we not report to Almalik before going on?"

The girl bit her lip, was about to speak; but Quamodian overrode her. "No!" he rasped. "You have waited too long already. Molly Zaldivar may be dying—may even be—" he did not finish the sentence.

Then they were at the center of the spiral. Quamodian glanced down, swallowed, looked at the girl —then tipped the flyer down into the central shaft.

Cautiously they dropped down the shaft, Quamodian's flyer first, the multiple grass-green citizen second, the pink cloud hovering timorously behind. Below them a misty, opalescent disk of pale light expanded slowly into a sphere, and they entered the great round chamber below the hill.

"Astonishing," breathed Clothilde Kwai Kwich.

The tardy cloud citizen sighed fearfully: "The energies are considerable! I am reluctant to come closer."

"Stay, then," grunted Quamodian, staring about. "I wonder—what is it? Do you have any information?"

The girl shook her head. "Some ancient military installation, I suppose. Perhaps from the days of the Plan of Man. The records no longer exist for much of that period. But that fusion fire!" She pointed at the cloud of opal mist that hung above the high steel platform. "What a source of energy! I almost believe that you are right, Monitor Quamodian. With power like that one might really attempt to create a star!"

Andy Quam chuckled sourly, but did not answer. Hands sweating on the flare controls, he dived to a foot or less above the water-stained floor of the sphere. The ripped and flattened orange-painted cab, the dismembered motor and tracks of the handling machine gave him an unpleasant start; something had thrown them about in rage, it seemed. And there were other fragments there among the torn and broken metal bits. A primitive white-painted food refrigerator? Quam did not recognize it at first, did not understand its purpose even then—but finally shook with the realization of what it meant: Molly Zalidvar had been here. The food could have been for no one but her.

But it too had been dropped or flung; the door

was twisted ajar, small packets of food were sprinkled across the wreckage. And beyond them, what was that crushed black shape that lay athwart the grating that attempted to carry seepage away?

Clothilde Kwai Kwich recognized it first: "A robot inspector!" she gasped. "Then—then it's all true!"

Rufe said complainingly, "True? Gosh, Miss Kwai Kwich, what've we been telling you all along? Of course it's true!"

It was too late for Andy Quam to feel triumph. He hardly heard the exchange. Eyes narrowed, thoughtful, he was darting the flyer's beams into every section of the vast sphere. There was nothing else to be seen. The wreckage on the floor, the spidery steel tower and its ominously glittering mist of fusion energy, the water-stained walls themselves. Nothing more.

Molly Zaldivar had been here, he was sure of that. But she was here no longer.

Where had she gone?

The nervous sigh of the cloud citizen interrupted him. "These energies," it whispered despairingly, "they are ionizing my gases, interfering with my particulate control. I must return to the surface."

"Go ahead," said Quam absently.

"Perhaps we should do the same," bayed the predator in the back seat. "This is dangerous!"

"In a minute," said Andy Quam. He was observing, remembering, analyzing. Dispassionately he realized, with a small surface part of his brain, that from the moment Molly Zaldivar's message had reached him, galaxies away, he had been allowing his love and his emotions to drive him. His carefully trained reasoning faculties, the trait of analysis and synthesis which was so basic a part of his indoctrination as a monitor, had been ignored.

But now he was using them again, and a picture was unfolding under his eyes, Cliff Hawk, rebel, adventurer, skilled transcience expert. The Reefer, callous misogynist. The two of them together in this place, given these energies, the months and even years of time when they had been left unsupervised.

It was all quite logical, he noted abstractly. Hawk's scientific hunger; the Reefer's loathing for humanity and, above all, the fusorian brotherhood; the people, the place, the facilities. They had used them to create a rogue, and in return the rogue had thrust them aside, or killed them, or ignored them.

But it had not ignored Molly Zaldivar.

The rogue was no longer present; its energies would have been detected by any of the citizens in the party. It had gone. And wherever it had gone, Quamodian felt certain, there would be Molly Zaldivar as well.

The girl monitor said hesitantly, "Andy. I mean, Monitor Quamodian . . ."

"Eh? What is it?"

"Perhaps the other citizens are right. I—I don't like the look of this place."

Quamodian frowned. Then a fearsome suspicion crossed his mind. "Clothilde! What was it the cloud said?"

"You mean the cit . . ."

"Yes! About the energies!"

"Why, it said they were ionizing gases. It has returned to the open air."

"Flyer!" cried Andy Quam. "Analyze those radiations! Quickly!"

The flyer said sulkily. "Thought you'd never ask. Sustained lethality, eight times permissible levels. Safe period at this distance, one hour. We have now been exposed to them for nineteen minutes, and I was going to give a warning alert in sixty seconds."

"Get us out of here!" ordered Andy Quam. "Fast!"

The flyer bucked, spun, drove upward toward the tunnel. Quamodian stared out the viewplate. The glowing deadly sphere of light flashed past his field of vision, then the tight spiral of the tunnel walls; but he did not see them.

Andy Quam was seeing something quite different, and far worse.

The radiation from that glittering mist of nuclear fire that had flamed for ages in the spherical cave was deadly.

The flyer's instruments had measured its intensity. They were reliable. Quamodian had installed and checked them himself. If they said that the maximum safe dose was one hour, then there was no question, give or take a minute or so, allowing for possible error.

It was not Quamodian's own safety that concerned him, nor Monitor Clothilde Kwai Kwich's, nor the boy's.

How long had Molly Zaldivar been held prisoner in that cave, soaking in those deadly rays?

Quamodian's calculation could be little more than a guess. But it was eighteen hours or more since she had been stolen from the little bedroom of Rufe's house. It was not sensible to suppose that less than half of that time had been spent in the cave.

And if it was in fact true that she had been there that long, or anything close to that long, Molly Zaldivar was already as good as dead.

XXIV

They burst out into the cold night air. And even in his fear and anguish Andy Quam stared incredulously at the sky.

Overhead lay a lacy net of blue and violet fire. Great pale slow lightnings of color writhed through the heavens, soundlessly and immense; they were so bright that trees cast shadows on the rocky hillside, blurred shadows of color that moved with the supple shifting of the aurora.

The carnivorous citizen thrust its long muzzle forward, past Quamodian's cheek. He felt its hot, faintly fishy breath on his ear as it whined softly, "This spectacle does not appear usual. Can you explain it?"

Quamodian said simply, "I think our own sun has gone rogue. I don't know why."

"But that's impossible," cried the girl. "Sol is not an intellectic body! No trace of volition has ever been detected!"

Quamodian spread his hands, indicating the violence of the aurora. "Then you explain it," he said.

The distant chorus of the grass-green spirals chimed in, "We have recorded reflected intensity of stellar emissions. They have approximately doubled. Three conjectures: One, that this star is prenova; improbable. Two, that previous soundings to determine intellect in this star have been in error; improbable. Three, that it has acquired volition."

"You mean it's gone rogue?" the girl demanded. "What probability do you give that?"

"No assessment," chanted the spirals. "No known data for comparison."

"Report to Almalik!" ordered the girl. "You, citizen! You have transcience facilities!"

But the spirals replied, "Our signals from Almalik are disordered. We cannot comprehend their meaning. Nor can we receive acknowledgment of our own reports."

Quamodian had had enough. "Forget Almalik!" he ordered. "And never mind about the sun, either; we can worry about that later. Right now I'm worried about a girl. A human girl named Molly Zaldivar. Perhaps she is somewhere nearby, with or without the rogue intellect. Can any of you detect her?"

Silence.

"Try!" roared Andy Quam. Then, sulkily, the predator citizen lifted its muzzle.

"For some time now," it bayed softly, the transcience receptor in Quamodian's ears converting it into words he could understand, "I have registered the presence of quarry on that far hill."

"Quarry?"

"An ancestral trait," the citizen explained. "It is a particular refinement of chemosampling in ambient air. What you call the sense of smell. But—is not

Senior Monitor Kwai Kwich 'human girl' and are not you 'human male,' Monitor Quamodian?"

"Certainly! What about it?"

"Then this quarry cannot be what you seek. It is male. And it is severely injured."

They skimmed over the pitted road, dropped toward the hillside where the carnivore citizen had scented a man. Its sense of smell had not been in error.

The man was the Reefer, huddled against the trunk of a bent evergreen tree. He looked gray and ill in the flickering colored lights of the aurora. One arm, badly swollen, was in a sling. He gazed up at the flyer apathetically as Quamodian jumped out.

"I want a word with you," Andy Quam shouted.

The Reefer growled hoarsely, "Make it short. I'm a sick man."

"Where is the rogue? Where is Molly Zaldivar?"

The Reefer shifted his weight awkwardly, flinching from the movement of his arm. "Gone. I don't know where."

"When?"

The Reefer shook his head wearily. Pale with pain, he pulled a short black stick from his pocket, gnawed the end off it and began chewing grimly. "A root that grows on the reefs," he said, his voice almost inaudible. "Filthy to chew, I guess, but it eases pain. It has always been my personal substitute for Almalik. When did the rogue go? I don't know. It dumped me here this afternoon. Couple hours ago something went on over there—" he gestured weakly at the hill that lay over the cave, "and I saw something bright in the sky."

"The aurora?" Quamodian demanded.

"No! That's been going on since dark. This was something else. I think—" his voice trailed off; he shook himself and finished, "I think the rogue is out in space. Maybe took the girl with him."

Monitor Clothilde Kwai Kwich interrupted. "Andy! This man is dying. I suggest we get him to a hospital."

The Reefer grinned painfully, working his lips for a second, then jetted a stream of black liquid at a rock. "Good idea, miss," he said. "Only it's too late for the hospital. I'm going to the church."

"Gosh, preacher!" breathed Rufe, wide-eyed behind Andy Quam in the shifting auroral lights. "Never thought *he'd* say that!"

"Never would," rumbled the Reefer, "if I had the choice. Knew it was coming. Your robot inspector told me weeks ago, 'Malignant fusorian virus,' he said, and acted like he was enjoying it—much as a robot can enjoy anything. And he said the Visitants could clear it up, but no doctor could. Expect he's right."

"So you're joining Almalik," said Andy Quam.

The Reefer shrugged bitterly, and winced from his slung arm. "I've tamed my last sleeth. My free life's ended." A spasm of pain whitened his face beneath the scars and the dirty beard. "Don't think I like it, Quamodian! But half my body's on fire."

"Good!" cried Andy Quam. "That's fine! Now, if you want a ride to Wisdom Creek, you can start paying the fare!"

The boy gasped, and even Clothilde Kwai Kwich darted a sudden incredulous look at Quamodian. The Reefer licked his lips, staring at Quamodian.

"What're you talking about? I'm too sick for jokes!"

"That's good, because I'm not joking. I'm going to leave you here to rot—unless you make it worth my while to take you in."

"How?"

"Easiest thing in the world," Quamodian said tightly. "Let's just start by telling me the truth about what you and Cliff Hawk were doing."

Under the many-hued gleam of the auroras the Reefer's eyes glowed whitely, furiously. If he had had the transcience powers of the sleeth, Andreas Quamodian would have been stunned or dead in that moment; there was madness in his look, and a rage that could destroy planets.

But it passed. The Reefer looked away. His jaws worked; he gulped, spat a thin black stream of the juice of his root and said, "Why not? Makes no difference any more, does it? After all, the Visitants will soon be burrowing in my brain and exposing all my secrets for Almalik to know. Might as well tell you now as have you find out that way—but let me sit down in your flyer, Quamodian. I'm telling the truth about being sick."

Andy Quam opened the bubble for him, and painfully the huge man sank into the cushions. The autonomic circuits of the flyer compensated for his weight and he sat bobbing slightly, looking down on them.

"Truth is," he said, "Cliff Hawk was only working for me. Insolent pup! I knew he thought he was pretty high and mighty, chasing after pure knowledge and all that stuff. But all I wanted was a cure for this virus. Ever since I picked it up on the reefs, more'n twenty years ago, it's been sleeping there inside me. I didn't mean for it to kill me, Quamodian. But I didn't mean to take on the Visitants, either."

He soothed his splinted arm with rough, blunt fingers, staring up at the many-hued sky. "I did like some of the things the Visitants had to offer, of course. Physical immortality, just about. A cure for this fusorian poison. Power—the rogues were my way of getting those things, without letting those parasites into my body. Hawk was just my engineer."

"So you knew Cliff Hawk was creating a rogue?" Quamodian leaned forward to search the Reefer's lax and bloodless face.

"Two rogues, Quamodian. The first got away." He grinned with a spasm of pain. "Looks like the other one did too!"

"I see," whispered Andy Quam, staring up at the angry aurora. "The first one entered our sun. Now it's rogue too!"

The Reefer shrugged.

Clothilde Kwai Kwich cried, "Monitor Quamodian! This must be reported at once. Since our citizens are not in contact with Almalik, we must return immediately to Wisdom Creek and report via the transflex station there."

"It's been reported already," said Andy Quam.

"Impossible! How could it be? We just found out . . ."

"By Rufe's parents. They knew about it, didn't they?" The boy nodded, looking pleased and excited. "And they've gone to Nuevo York to pass the word along."

The Reefer scratched his ribs cautiously, winced and groaned. "So that's about it, right? Now how about taking me in to Wisdom Creek?"

"Not just yet," said Andy Quam, deadly quiet. "One more question. What about Molly Zaldivar?"

"That witless little thing! She ruined Cliff Hawk. In love with her, he was; she tried to stop him, and messed everything up."

He gasped and leaned forward, clutching his chest. "But I don't know where she is now, Quamodian," he moaned. "Please! Isn't that enough? Won't you take me in before this thing kills me?"

On the way to Wisdom Creek Andy Quam used the flyer's circuits to contact the control dome for priorities. "Thirty-minute delay on all messages, Monitor Quamodian," said the dome. "I will inform you when your circuits can be cleared."

Grim-lipped, Andy Quam ordered the flyer to the Starchurch. Now that he knew what was wrong with the sun his responsibility was at an end. Almalik would cope with the problem—somehow—or Almalik would fail; Quamodian didn't care. At that moment the only thing on his mind was Molly Zaldivar, stolen into space by the rogue and doomed to early death by the lethal rays of the old power source in the cavern. As for the Reefer, Quamodian didn't care in the slightest whether he lived or died.

Yet there was a sort of grandeur in what happened at the Starchurch. They were greeted by the new robot inspector, his egg-shaped black body bobbing with excitement at the presence of so many illustrious visitors. Even though this was not a Starday, a circle of the saved were kneeling on that wide floor beneath the imaged suns of Almalik, and Quamodian and Monitor Clothilde Kwai Kwich led the procession that brought the limping, sullen figure of the Reefer to the Visitants. Behind him the carnivorous citizen, the green spiral citizen and the cloud brought up the rear.

The kneeling worshippers chanted their praises of Almalik. Then Juan Valdivar stood up to ask the Reefer the statutory question—if he understood the nature of symbiotic life; if he had chosen of his own free will to accept the fusorian symbiotes in his body, blood, brain and bone; if he understood that this choice was made forever.

To each question, the Reefer croaked, "I do."

He knelt, and the inhabited saved ones knelt with him, their golden brands glowing in the gloom. They chanted again, their voices rolling solemnly against the mighty dome that held the thirteen suns of Almalik.

The Reefer gasped a sudden protesting cry.

He rose half to his feet, turned with a sudden look of wild alarm, then pitched forward on his damaged arm.

Quamodian heard a sharp, hissing crackle. Fine golden sparks were dancing up from the glowing marks on the bodies and faces of the saved ones, floating delicately toward the prone body of the Reefer. They flew together, gathering into a tiny cloud of golden fire that hovered over him.

The yellow fireball sank hissing into his skin.

An arm of it darted around his body, touched his cheek, retreated to rejoin the rest. The air was suddenly heavy with the sweet reek of the Visitants.

The Reefer's moans subsided.

Then the chanting ended. He stirred, opened his eyes, stood up easily and came to shake Andreas Quamodian's hand.

"Thanks, friend," his great voice boomed. A serene and gentle smile had fallen over his scarred ferocious face. The star of the Visitants now glowed faintly above his ragged beard. "All my pain is gone."

Juan Valdivar came to take his hand. "You are saved now. You'll feel no pain again," he said solemnly.

The control dome had been in touch with Almalik. But there were difficulties. Quamodian blazed, "What difficulties? I must communicate with Almalik at once—go there as soon as possible!"

"Regret," sang the control dome sweetly. "It is a matter of priorities."

"That's what I demand, emergency priority!"

"But Monitor Quamodian," sang the control dome, "when you arrived yesterday you stated the emergency was here."

"It *was* here. Now I have new facts! I expect a most serious danger to the suns of Almalik!"

Clothilde Kwai Kwich whispered, "Andy, may I speak to him? Perhaps he will listen—" But Quamodian froze her with a glare. She subsided without comment. She had become a softer, more feminine person since the visit to the cave, the discovery that Andy Quam's fears were not groundless.

"State these facts," the monitor rapped out melodiously.

"They are already available to Almalik," said Quamodian. "They exist in the mind of a man called the Reefer who has just received the Visitants. I wish to be on hand among the stars of Almalik, to assist with the interpretation and use of this new information."

He did not add his more urgent private reason; it would have been of no use, since it was not the sort of thing that would influence the control dome's transcience patterns. But he clung to a wild, despairing hope that Molly Zaldivar might appear with her captor, somewhere about the multiple suns of Almalik. If she did, Quamodian wanted to be there.

"Moment," sang the monitor dome. Andy Quam shifted uneasily in the seat of the flyer.

Clothilde Kwai Kwich frowned thoughtfully. "*We* have priorities," she stated, as if to no one.

"What about it?" Quam demanded.

"Nothing, Andy. Except that the rest of us can go to Almalik at once and plead your cause."

"Agree," chanted the chorus of the grass-green spirals. "Impatient. Urgent. Suggest no delay."

And the cloud citizen sighed, "There exist great forces deployed against Almalik. It is necessary to prepare immediately."

Quamodian said stubbornly, "Do what you like. I am going anyway."

Clothilde looked at him doubtfully, but said nothing. She was saved the need to, anyway; the control dome spoke in all their ears, through the little communicator plugs:

"Monitor Quamodian, your request is denied, Senior Monitor Kwai Kwich, your priorities, and those of your party, are withdrawn. There can be no travel to that destination now."

The news struck them all with consternation. The green spirals whirled furiously in their interlocking orbits, their collective thoughts a babel of whispered fear and excitement, just below the threshhold of comprehensibility for the others. The predator citizen whined mournfully and edged closer to the boy, Rufe, who stared wide-eyed at Andy Quam. The pinkly glowing cloud citizen whispered somber predictions about the disasters that lay ahead, and Clothilde Kwai Kwich's hand crept out, unnoticed, to take the hand of Andy Quam.

"Why?" he demanded furiously. "We are monitors! We cannot be denied priority rights!"

"All priorities are withdrawn," said the control dome somberly. "Our headquarters report anomalous astronomical phenomena among the planets and multiple suns of Almalik. Robot inspector, please clarify."

Unnoticed, the black egg-shaped form of the robot had drifted across the square toward them. Its oval sensor was cool and bright and blank. Its high voice hummed: "That is correct, Monitor Quamodian. The outer planet of Almalik Thirteen has suddenly stopped in its orbit. It is moving on a collision course toward its primary at many times the normal acceleration of gravity."

Quamodian's eyes narrowed. His mind whirled with chaotic flashes of foreboding. Molly was there! He was certain of it now, and certain that he must get to her. "Not surprising!" he barked, surprising himself. "That is precisely what I hoped to prevent! I must get there at once to limit the damage, avoid it if I still can."

"Impossible, Monitor Quamodian," the robot

whirred. "The collision of the anomalous planet with Almalik Thirteen is expected to occur within a few hours. All transflex facilities are in use for the evacuation of the threatened planets. Even so, they are inadequate. Only a fraction of the population can be saved. Under these circumstances, no incoming travel is permitted."

Clothilde Kwai Kwich gasped. The predator citizen lifted his snout and emitted a long, mourning howl.

Quamodian stammered, "But—but I must go there! To help! It is still possible to do something . . ."

The robot did not respond. Its bright black case hung motionless.

Rufe whispered fearfully, "Preacher, what's the matter? Is it dead?"

Quamodian shook his head, staring. The robot's plasma sensor flickered, darkened, went out. Three thick black effector whips slid out of its body shell and dangled limply below it, brushing the dusty pavement of the square.

"Robot Inspector?" Quamodian called querulously. Beside him the girl whispered, "There's something terribly wrong! It's out of communication entirely."

But abruptly the effectors snapped back into the case. The sensor glowed again.

"We have received a further instruction from headquarters," it hummed. "The information states that a powerful rogue invader has destroyed the native intellects in two of the suns of Almalik. The invader has established its own transcience patterns

195

in these suns, and it is now attacking the planets of Almalik Thirteen."

Quamodian caught a sudden, rasping breath.

"Call Cygnus!" he demanded.

"Sacred Almalik, spokesman star of Cygnus, is calling here," the robot's high whine interrupted him. "Your transflex travel priority has been approved. You and your party may depart from the Wisdom Creek transflex station at once."

XXV

Light-millennia away, the rogue's consciousness grew and sharpened in the heat of a cosmic fury. The huge sentience of stripped electrons and plasma soliloquized to itself like a stellar Hamlet:

My seas boil dry . . . my magma bleeds from glowing wounds . . . my core itself is shattered by those savage plasma spears . . . still I hurl myself toward the great white sun ahead . . .

The inner planets of the sun spread wider in their orbits as it approached. They began flashing backward past it; it was hours only now until they, and all the space about, would be dissolved in the blazing debris of the sun the rogue was about to destroy.

And still the sun did not resist.

Swelling vast ahead of the rogue, it lay serenely white, beautiful and quiet, undisturbed by the rogue's attack.

By now the rogue was ancient and mature—in its own terms at least; it had existed and learned through billions of cycles of its picosecond reflexes. It had learned a full complement of "emotions," or at any rate of those polarizing tropisms which did for it what the glandular by-products called emotions did for human beings. It had learned anger, and the calm pride of the target sun called forth anger in the rogue:

If it would only recognize me! If it would only admit causing the sun of Earth to strike at me! If it would offer some apology for deceiving me, for its contempt of me—then perhaps I could yet stop my blow . . .

But it ignored him.

The rogue was not entirely ignored. Though the great white star blazed on passionlessly, benevolently, still the rogue found itself the target for great forces from elsewhere. Another sun of Almalik had joined the attack upon it. The blue companion of the golden giant stabbed at it with a twisting shaft of plasma, a monstrous snake of glowing ions and tran-science energy, which pierced to the rogue's heart, withdrew and jabbed again.

An agony of meta-pain jolted the rogue to its innermost plasma swirl; but it was not destroyed. It gathered its forces and sought for a weapon to hurl back the thrust of the blue star.

And it found one. Passing by the great fifth planet of the unresisting white sun, the rogue reached out with its plasma arms to snatch a string of moons. It gathered them to itself, fused their shattered mass into its own body, linked their electrons into its transcience patterns. With its new mass it strengthened its defenses.

And secure in its new strength, it drew more strength from the attacking stars themselves. It sucked their transcience energies, through the blue bolts and the golden ones, tightened its transflection fields and hurled its new mass always faster toward the maddening white star that glowed on, contemptuous of all the rogue could do.

And that phase of the battle ended.

Though the rogue had never struck back at the twin attacking giants, they were beaten.

Their plasma coils had exhausted even their giant strength. The coils withdrew, collapsed, disintegrated. The blue giant shrank and dimmed; its golden companion swelled and reddened.

And then they were both dead. Their fusion fires still blazed on—but mindlessly now; the intellects that had animated them were drained empty.

Sentience had fled from them. Anger and fear and purpose had gone. The blue star swelled again, the golden companion shrank back to normal size; they had become merely globes of reacting nuclear gas, normal atomic engines no longer controlled by any transcience intellect.

It was a clear victory for the rogue—but its major enemy, the bright white star in its path, was still the same.

It was not defeated. If it was even threatened, it gave no sign.

The rogue felt its vast quiet mind watching, alert but strangely unafraid. It was anomalous, the rogue considered, that the target star did not request mercy, or a discussion of terms. Anomalous—and some-how disturbing.

But the rogue would not be deterred from its purpose. It plunged on to smash the white star and its haughty pride. It sought and found new fuel for its vengeance. Passing a cloud of asteroids, it swept them up and added them to its mass. It reached ahead to gather in the barren satellite of the fourth planet, and crushed and fused the new mass into its own as it sought to crush and fuse all the suns of Almalik.

Already in anticipation, it tasted the acrid joy of victory and destruction.

Thirteen suns would die or be driven to mindless burning. A hundred planets, and a thousand inhabited worldlets would be destroyed. A million billion living things would go up in white-hot plasma as the stars died . . .

And among them, thought the rogue with a bleak stab of pain, would be the trivial living blob of organized matter called Molly Zaldivar.

I do not wish Molly Zaldivar to die. She must die. I will not save her. But I do not wish her to die, because I love her.

In its deadly plunge toward the white star it sent thin threads of plasma effectors ahead to seek her out. Its sensor filaments ranged the cubic miles of void, and found her at last, still on the sleeth, far ahead of the rogue and dropping toward the atmosphere of the third planet. The arm of the golden giant that had freed her from the rogue was gone now, with its master's death; but Molly Zaldivar still lived.

And felt the rogue's delicate tendril touch.

She looked up unerringly toward the point in space where his massed energies were driving the planet down to its primary. "Monster?" she whispered.

The rogue was silent. It merely watched, and listened.

"Monster," she said, more confident now, "I know you're there. I don't mind."

She was silent for a moment, leaning forward over the sleek black skin of the sleeth, staring toward the cloudy world below. "You've done so much harm, monster," she sighed, "I wish—and yet you've tried to be good to me. Monster, I'm so sorry that you must make war on Almalik!"

The rogue did not answer. But it probed her interior spectrum of thoughts and energies, registered the dark shadow of sadness and, with it, a pale golden glow of—of what? Love? Fondness at least, the rogue considered.

It contracted its tendril to the merest whisper, content only to observe her, while it considered. Its strength was so immeasurably greater than her own that it could lift her from the sleeth in an instant. The energies that had hurled planets about and slain stars could fold both her and the sleeth back into its own fused and glowing mass effortlessly, carrying them with it into the collision with the proud white star ahead.

But it did not.

It watched her carefully, but without interfering, as she darted, secure in the sleeth's shimmering transflection fields, into the ionized border layers of the third planet's atmosphere and dropped swiftly toward the cities on its surface.

The third planet was a blue-green world, and beautiful. It was a world of peaceful seas and friendly continents. Dazzling cities dwelt along its oceans and rivers, inhabited by all the many kinds of creatures that were companions of Almalik.

The rogue watched her drop into the towering spires of one of the cities. It was not yet too late; it could sweep her up even there, and bring her back in the effortless recoil of one of its plasma arms.

But it stayed its energies. It merely watched, as it drove on toward the collision, now little more than an hour off, which would sear and melt this world, and destroy the organized mass of matter that was Molly Zaldivar.

XXVI

The flyer, with its organic passengers and trailed by the green spirals and the pink cloud citizen, fell endlessly through the transflection distances, and emerged into the exit port of Kaymar, crown city of the planet of Kaymar, central world of Almalik.

Clothilde Kwai Kwich's hand tightened in consternation on Andy Quam's arm. Beside him the boy gasped. "Preacher! Looks like we've come to a bad place!"

The great central dome of the city seethed with citizens of all kinds. Many were human, in this central city of the worlds of Almalik; calm Terrestrials, bronzed giants from the reefs. But there were citizens in a myriad shapes and in no shapes at all, liquid citizens and gaseous citizens, citizens that had no form of matter to clothe the bare energies that constituted their beings. The diaphragm of the transflex cube behind them was already contracting on a full load of refugees lucky enough to be on their way to some other world. The shouts, cries, hissing whistles, electronic pulses and other signals of the countless thousands who had not yet been so lucky added up to a vast chorus of pleas for help. Twenty crystal citizens hung just before them, their razor-sharp edges of bright blue transparency flashing in the suns of Almalik. Quam dropped the flyer to the ramp, opened the door and led the way, ducking under the crystal citizens.

"Got to get out of this crush," he panted. "Headquarters of the Companions of the Star is just over here—I think . . ."

Clothilde Kwai Kwich cried breathlessly, "Yes, Andy! They'll still be functioning; we'll go there, and—" but she had no breath to finish. It was all they could do to urge their way through the incredible press of citizens. There was neither violence nor outright panic; these were not the enemy. But there were so many of them, so many countless thousands more than the transflex cube could evacuate in the few score minutes left, and backed by so many thousands of thousands more that had not yet managed to make their way even into the central dome of the city. They were orderly. They were brave. But each of them knew that most of them were doomed.

They fought their way to a clear space and paused

for breath. The carnivore citizen was the least affected of them; he glanced at young Rufe and bayed a laughing comment which the translators in Quamodian's ear rendered as: "Let the cub ride my shoulders! We'll never make it any other way."

"Naw!" flamed Rufe. "I can keep up if you can. Come on, preacher, let's do what we came to do!"

The pinkly glowing cloud citizen was worst damaged of the party. Little cloudlets of his material had been detached; some were still floating after him, rejoining the central mass of his being; others were hopelessly lost in the crush behind them. The grass-green spirals had merely tightened their orbits, maintaining exact spacing and speeds.

"All right," said Andy Quam. "Let's go!"

But a great shout from the dome behind them made them turn.

Every citizen, warm-blooded or cold, humanoid or amorphous, was staring upward, through the crystal ceiling of the dome, with ten thousand thousand eyes, photoreceptors, radar scanners, sensors of every description.

There, streaked like a child's bright daub on the calm blue skies of Kaymar, hung the bright and glittering globe of the invading rogue star. Lightnings played about its blazing body as it shot across the sky, its motion visible even though its distance was many millions of miles.

Andy Quam tore his eyes away. "Come on," he muttered. "We've got even less time than I thought."

The Grand Hall of the Companions of the Star was empty. The thirteen suns of Almalik blazed down from the ceiling on an auditorium that could seat thousands, and now held no one at all.

Senior Monitor Clothilde Kwai Kwich said dolefully, "I can't understand. I thought here at least we'd find someone who could help . . ."

The chant of the grass-green spirals sounded in Andy Quam's ears: "No indications! No operative functions being performed! This construct not inhabited!"

The boy clutched Quamodian's arm. "But, preacher," he said. "Almalik told us to come here. Didn't he?"

Quamodian said, "He gave us permission. Directly. Yes." He turned, searching the vast room with his eyes. "But perhaps something has happened."

The weary sigh of the cloud citizen whispered: "There exists a large-scale entity which is observing us."

Quamodian flung himself into a chair, trying to think. Time was so short! He had counted on finding the order of Companions of the Star still functioning. Perhaps it had not been realistic, but in his mind he had expected to find the great hall thronged with worshippers, the many offices and administrative sections busy about the endless tasks of Almalik. If he had thought at all, he had thought that a robot monitor of a citizen would have greeted them at the entrance, led them directly to someone in supreme authority, received his information about the rogue— and acted. Acted in time to save this world, and all the worlds of Almalik.

He had not expected that the building would be empty.

The others were waiting quietly for him to act. He

realized that, right or wrong, he would have to make the decisions for all of them. And there was less time with every passing clock-tick . . .

He stood up. "All right," he said, "we'll go back to the transflex cube. Perhaps the monitor there can help us."

"Through that mob, preacher? Impossible!" cried the boy.

"Impossible or not, that's what we'll have to do. Unless you have a better idea . . ."

But then, as they turned to leave, a Voice rumbled softly in their ears.

"Wait," it said.

They froze where they stood. The girl looked imploringly at Andy Quam. She did not speak, but her lips formed a word: "Almalik?"

He nodded; and the Voice spoke again:

"Behold," it said, and the great dome lifted on its transflection forces to reveal the splendor of the heavens of Almalik themselves. It was daytime now; the glittering stars that the dome was designed to reveal could not be seen. But the bright smear of the invader was there, blighting the beauty of the calm clouds. And near it in the sky, dropping toward them . . .

"It's Miss Zaldivar!" shouted the boy. "Look, preacher! It's her and the sleeth!"

They were in that great hall for less than a quarter of an hour, and in all that time Quamodian could not afterward remember taking a breath. He was overpowered by the immense majesty of Almalik himself, brooding over them, watching and helping. Even the nearness of the girl he had crossed half a universe to find could not break him free from the spell of that immortal and immense star.

Though what was said was surely catastrophic enough to rouse him to action; for Molly Zaldivar, she said, was dying.

"Dear Andy," she whispered across the vast gulf of the chamber, her voice warm and affectionate in his ears. "No! Don't come any closer to me. I'm charged with radiations, Andy dear—the old ones from the Plan of Man machines, new ones that our little monster-star used to try to save my life. Or to give me life again; because I was dead. Anyway, if you come near me now it will be your death . . ."

Even so, he rose to run toward her; but she stopped him with a gesture. "Please," she whispered. "Now. What was it that you came from Earth to tell?"

He stammered out the story the Reefer had told him, while Clothilde Kwai Kwich and the boy, one on each side of him, stood silent and awed. Molly Zaldivar listened gravely, her face composed though her eyes widened, then danced, as she saw how Clothilde's hand sought his.

Then she said, "Thank you, Andy. You've always been the best friend I could ever hope to have. I . . ."

Her composure almost broke for a moment, but she controlled herself, and smiled. "I don't mind leaving this world much, dear Andy. But I do mind leaving you."

And then she was gone, mounting once more toward the sky on the great, patient back of the sleeth, while the enormous dome of Almalik swung majestically back into place to blot her out.

XXVII

The rogue sensed the fear in that distant watcher, the fear of a father for a threatened son. It thought to call for help, but the distance was a thousand times too far. Even here, its thin thread of sensor had been snapped; it had lost Molly Zaldivar and her sleeth.

It tried to find them again for many picoseconds, but in vain. Some force larger than itself had shut her off, blinded it to her activities. A sense that in a human might have been called foreboding filled the rogue; but it had no time for even meta-emotions; it was driving ever closer to its enemy sun, and it needed all its forces for the task ahead.

The third planet had fallen far behind it now. It flashed through the orbit of the second planet, now hidden from it at inferior conjunction by the expanding white sun. The great white disk grew ahead of it.

Still the star ignores my attack. It refuses to resist. It offers no apology for the attacks it has made on me through its lesser stars. Still it is watching—mocking me . . .

"Monster! Stop for me."

The thin filament of the rogue's probing sensor was alive again, carrying a message for it. The rogue energized its perceptions and saw that Molly Zaldivar was pursuing, racing after it on the black and shining sleeth. There was a power flowing from her that the rogue could not quite recognize, but that made it uneasy, unsure of itself. The feeble human figure of organized matter that was the girl should not have been able to dispose such powers. Not even with the energies the rogue itself had bestowed on her; not when her life was close to an end, and all her accumulated strengths were being disposed at once.

The rogue considered for some nanoseconds the possibility that these forces came from its enemy, Almalik. But it dismissed the possibility. It simply did not matter. Contact was only minutes away. Already the thin solar atmosphere was boiling around it. It did not stop, perhaps could not stop; the gathered mass of its planetary body was plunging too fast to be diverted now.

But it sent a message through its plasma effector, shaking the thin atmosphere that the sleeth carried with it through space. "What do you want, Molly Zaldivar?" its tiny voice piped. "Do you love me now?"

Her answer sent a seismic tremor through the core of the planet it had made its body: "Love you, monster? I don't know. I cannot imagine it. And yet—yes, perhaps I do. If it matters . . ."

The rogue shook in its mad plunge. Its boiling seas loosed huge clouds of vapor as, for a moment, its grasp slackened; lightnings played through its tortured skies. But Molly was still speaking:

"But I have no life left to love anyone, monster. My body is dying, and I must tell you something.

Monster! Please listen. *Almalik is not your enemy.*"

A shock of doubt shattered the rogue's great joy.

"Listen monster! Almalik never hurt you. Almalik has renounced all violence. He could not harm you, nor any sentient thing. Ever!"

Rage shook the rogue now. The crustal rocks of its planetary body snapped and white-hot magma spewed forth. In the air around Molly Zaldivar its tiny voice shrieked: "Lies! Lies again! The sun of Earth that tried to kill me was Almalik's vassal. Its twin stars that tried to kill me again—they were Almalik's companions!"

But Molly Zaldivar's voice came strongly. "No, monster. I lied to you once, yes. Because I was afraid of you. But Almalik has never lied, nor has he tried to harm you. The sun of Earth that struck you—it was your own brother!"

The rogue called back the huge effector that it had lashed out to strike her. Puzzled, its shrill voice repeated, "Brother?"

"Yes, your brother! Another synthetic sentience, made before you. It occupied the sun of Earth and tried to destroy you—came here before you, and tried to destroy you again through the twin stars of Almalik. But you defeated it, monster. And now it is gone, and you must stop before you destroy great Almalik!"

The rogue paused, while its sentient plasma revolved the startling new concept. "Brother?" its tiny voice whispered again. A dreadful doubt shivered through its core.

If it were wrong, it thought—if it were wrong, then it was doing a dreadful and irrevocable deed.

For if it were wrong, then Almalik had always

been its friend. And it was within minutes of destroying Almalik forever.

Methodically, patiently, the rogue rebuilt its net of sensors, threw out probes to scan the patient white star before it—so close now, and so vulnerable!—and all of space around. Its velocity, hard driven and accelerated through hundreds of millions of miles, was huge. Unstoppable. It had thrown its energies in profligate abandon into thrusting the dead planet toward the white star. It was simply too late to stop.

With care and speed it calculated possible trajectories to divert its own plunge, not to stop it—for that was utterly impossible now—but simply to deflect it enough to miss the star and plunge on into the dark space beyond . . .

Impossible. It was too late.

Well, then: to pass through the star's corona, destroying itself in the process, of course, and working great havoc with the star's internal energy balance, but leaving most of it intact . . .

Also impossible. Also too late.

In what passed in it for desperation, the rogue computed its chance of plunging through the skin of the star but on a tangent that would miss the core, leave the star wounded and erupting with enormous violence, but perhaps not entirely destroyed . . .

Also impossible, and finally impossible. Its energies were too great, its time of collision too near. It would strike the white sun almost dead on, whatever the rogue did now. And rogue and white star together would erupt in the ultimate violence of a supernova, destroying themselves and everything for a light-year or more around.

I regret, thought the rogue. *I feel pity. For Molly*

Zaldivar. For Almalik. For all the myriads of beings on Almalik's doomed planets. And for me.

It sent out a message on the thin, stretched filament of energy with which it had been in contact with Molly Zaldivar, to say that there was no longer any hope.

But it could not make contact.

Once again it searched all of space nearby, seeking Molly Zaldivar and the sleeth. Uselessly. Somehow, Molly Zaldivar was gone.

The patterns of energy that made up the essential being of the rogue were shaken with grief and pain. Despairing, it thrust with all the energies it possessed at the calm white disk of its target sun, now so near and so vulnerable. Great spouts of flame boiled from the star below it; the rogue's own planetary body split and shattered in the violence of its effort to undo what it had done. But it was no use. The fragments of its planet, continental in size, massive as worldlets themselves, drove on unchecked.

Look, little one. Take that blue star. Use its energies, if you will.

The rogue darted out sensors in all directions, seeking the source of that soundless, gentle voice. The sensors found nothing. But the rogue knew where it came from: it was Almalik, speaking to it from the enormous, swelling, flame-ringed solar disk so near below.

The blue star?

Experimentally the rogue threw out a sensor toward it. It was empty, untenanted since it had destroyed the mad sentience that had inhabited it. It was waiting for it.

211

Something helped the rogue, something to which it could not put a name: not merely Almalik, not just the star it was so close to destroying, but a congeries of sentiences, a pooled strength of living and stellar creatures, all urging the rogue on, supporting it, giving it help.

It drove along the lines of its sensor and entered into the waiting star.

New energies flooded its webs of sentience. The resources of a giant stellar furnace were now its own to command.

It reached out to the planet it had abandoned, hurtling down on the white star, grasped it with the mighty plasma arms of its new body. White arms from Almalik himself joined the rogue—and with them, golden arms. The rogue puzzled over that for a few electron-orbits; surely the golden star was dead, unable to take part.

Yet it was taking part. The golden arms linked with the blue and white ones, and together, smoothly, strongly, with infinite speed they pulled the planet aside.

The planet did not survive those mighty forces; it crumbled into a million billion fragments, streaming past the great white orb of Almalik and heading out into space on cometary orbits.

But it had missed. Almalik was safe.

And the rogue had time to realize what it had gained, in the might of its new stellar body—and what it had lost. It sensed the joy, the proud approval, of that far-off fatherly watcher—which was now more akin than ever, but no longer all rogue.

The great tolling chorus of the stars welcomed it

into brotherhood. *Join us, brother,* said a great collective voice. *Be one with us. Be one with all things that share the bonds of mind. Be one with Almalik.*

And a part of the rogue rejoiced, and a part of it ached with an unpracticed grief for Molly Zaldivar, doomed to death in her frail human body, lost forever.

The slow, gentle voice held a hint of amusement, and wry pity. *Look, brother,* it said. *You gave her your strength. We gave her our empty sun for a home.*

And the rogue struck out, unbelieving, with a bright blue plasma sensor toward the golden star; and it met the rogue's sensor with one of its own. Gold thread and blue touched and joined, while the stars watched and rejoiced.

The voice that spoke to the rogue was not a human voice, but there was something of humanity about it—something soft and merry, something very like the voice of Molly Zaldivar and dear.

"Hello, monster," it said. "Welcome. Welcome forever."

Frederik Pohl

"Frederik Pohl is practically required reading for any science fiction fan worthy of the name —and an excellent reason for becoming one!"

N.Y. Herald Tribune

DRUNKARD'S WALK
SLAVE SHIP
A PLAGUE OF PYTHONS
TOMORROW TIMES SEVEN
TURN LEFT AT THURSDAY
THE ABOMINABLE EARTHMAN

With new Robert Foster covers—75¢

EXCITING SCIENCE FICTION FROM
THE BALLANTINE LIST

Uniformly priced at 75¢ each
(Plus 5¢ per book mailing charge)

To order by mail, list the titles you want, add your address with zip code, and enclose 80¢ per title. Send to: Dept. CS, Ballantine Books, 36 West 20th Street, New York, New York 10003.

In Science Fiction
Ballantine Books Brings You
the Best of the Established Authors
and the Most Exciting New Writers

BY ARTHUR C. CLARKE
IN BALLANTINE BOOKS EDITIONS